Natalie quickly disguised another swallow. "You want more than one hundred thousand pounds?" she asked in a voice that sounded too high—squeaky almost.

Angelo looked at her, his eyes meshing with hers in a lockdown that made the silence throb with palpable tension. She felt it moving up her spine, vertebra by vertebra. She felt it on her skin, the ghosting of goose bumps fluttering along her flesh. She felt it—shockingly—between her thighs, as if he had reached down and touched her there.

He didn't say a word. He didn't need to. She could read the subtext of that dark mocking gaze. He didn't care about the money. It wasn't money he wanted. He had more than enough of his own.

Natalie knew exactly what he wanted. She had known it the minute she had stepped into his office and locked gazes with him.

He wanted her.

All about the author...
Melanie Milburne

From as soon as **MELANIE MILBURNE** could pick up a pen she knew she wanted to write. It was when she picked up her first Harlequin Mills & Boon novel at seventeen that she realized she wanted to write romance. Distracted for a few years by meeting and marrying her own handsome hero, surgeon husband Steve, and having two boys, plus completing a master's of education and becoming a nationally ranked athlete (masters swimming) she decided to write. Five submissions later she sold her first book and is now a multi-published, award-winning USA TODAY bestselling author. In 2008 she won the Australian Readers Association's most popular category/series romance and in 2011 she won the prestigious Romance Writers of Australia R*BY Award.

Melanie loves to hear from her readers via her website, www.melaniemilburne.com.au, or on Facebook, http://www.facebook.com/pages/Melanie-Milburne/351594482609.

Other titles by Melanie Milburne available in eBook:

Harlequin Presents®

   3038—HIS POOR LITTLE RICH GIRL
   3080—DESERVING OF HIS DIAMONDS
      (*The Outrageous Sisters*)
   3086—ENEMIES AT THE ALTAR
      (*The Outrageous Sisters*)

Melanie Milburne

SURRENDERING ALL BUT HER HEART

HARLEQUIN®

entertain, enrich, inspire™

Recycling programs
for this product may
not exist in your area.

ISBN-13: 978-0-373-13111-2

SURRENDERING ALL BUT HER HEART

Copyright © 2012 by Melanie Milburne

www.Harlequin.com

Printed in U.S.A.

SURRENDERING ALL BUT HER HEART

CHAPTER ONE

'YOU'LL *have to see him.*'

Natalie could still hear the desperation and pleading in her mother's tone even as she pressed the call button for the lift leading up to Angelo Bellandini's swish London office. The words had taken up residence in her head. They had kept her awake for the last forty-eight hours. They had accompanied her like oversized baggage on the train all the way from her home in Edinburgh. They had clickety-clacked over the tracks until they had been like a mind-numbing mantra in her head.

'You'll have to see him. You'll have to see him. You'll have to see him.'

Not that she *hadn't* seen him in the last five years. Just about every newspaper and online blog had a photo or information about the playboy heir to the Bellandini fortune. Angelo Bellandini's fast-living lifestyle was the topic of many an online forum. His massive wealth—of which, to his credit, only half was inherited; the other half had been acquired through his own hard work— made him a force to be reckoned with.

And now she *had to reckon with him, on behalf of her wayward younger brother and his foolish actions.*

A prickle of apprehension fluttered like a faceless,

fast-footed creature down the length of her spine as she stepped into the glass and chrome capsule of the lift. Her hand shook slightly as she reached for the correct floor button.

Would Angelo even agree to see her, given the way she had walked out of his life five years ago? Would he hate her as much as he had once loved her? Would the passion and desire that had once burned in his dark brown gaze now be a blaze of hatred instead?

Her insides shifted uneasily as she stepped out of the lift and approached the reception area. Having grown up with comfortable wealth, she should not be feeling so intimidated by the plush and elegant surroundings. But when they had first met Angelo had never revealed to her the extent of his family fortune. To her he had been just a hard-working, handsome Italian guy, studying for a Master's degree in business. He had gone to considerable lengths to conceal his privileged background—but then, who was she to talk?

She had revealed even less about hers.

'I'm afraid Signor Bellandini is unavailable at present,' his receptionist said in a crisp, businesslike tone in response to Natalie's request. 'Would you like to make an appointment for some other time?'

Natalie looked at the model-gorgeous young woman, with her perfectly smooth blonde hair and clear china-blue eyes, and felt her already flagging self-esteem plummet like an anchor to the basement. Even though in the lift she had reapplied lip-gloss and run her fingers through her nondescript flyaway brown hair, it was hardly the same as being professionally groomed. She was aware her clothes looked as if they had been slept in, even though she hadn't slept a wink for the last twenty-four hours, and that her normally peaches and cream complexion was grey with worry. There were damson-coloured shadows under her eyes and her cheeks had a hollow look to them. But then that happened every year at this time, and had done so since she was seven years old.

She straightened her shoulders with iron-strong resolve. She was not going to leave without seeing Angelo, even if she had to wait all day. 'Tell Signor Bellandini I'm only in London for the next twenty-four hours.' She handed her personal business card over the counter, as well as the card of the hotel she had booked for the night. 'I can be contacted on that mobile number or at my hotel.'

The receptionist glanced at the cards and then raised her eyes to Natalie's. 'You're Natalie Armitage?' she asked. 'The Natalie Armitage of Natalie Armitage Interiors?'

'Er...yes.'

The receptionist's eyes sparkled with delight. 'I have some of your sheets and towels,' she said. 'I just adored your last spring collection. Because of me, all of my friends now have your stuff. It's so feminine and fresh. So original.'

Natalie smiled politely. 'Thank you.'

The receptionist leaned towards the intercom. 'Signor Bellandini?' she said. 'A Miss Natalie Armitage is here to see you. Would you like me to squeeze her in before your next client or make another appointment for later this afternoon?'

Natalie's heart stalled in that infinitesimal moment before she heard his voice. Would he sound surprised to find she was here in person? Annoyed? Angry?

'No,' he said evenly, his deep baritone and sexy accent like a silky caress on her skin. 'I will see her now.'

The receptionist led the way down an expansive corridor and smiled as she came to a door bearing a brass plaque with Angelo's name on it. 'You're very lucky,' she said in a conspiratorial undertone. 'He doesn't normally see clients without an appointment. Most people have to wait weeks to see him.' Her eyes sparkled again. 'Maybe he wants to slip between your sheets, so to speak?'

Natalie gave a weak smile and stepped through the door the receptionist had opened. Her eyes went straight to where Angelo was seated, behind a mahogany desk that seemed to have a football field of carpet between it and the door that had just clicked shut, like the door of a prison cell, behind her.

Her throat tightened. She tried to unlock it by swallowing, but it still felt as if a puffer fish was lodged halfway down.

He looked as staggeringly gorgeous as ever—maybe even more so. The landscape of his face had barely changed, apart from two deep grooves that bracketed his unsmiling mouth. His raven-black hair was shorter than it had been five years ago, but it still curled lushly against the collar of his light blue business shirt. His face was cleanly shaven, but the dark pinpricks of persistent masculine stubble were clearly visible along his lean cheeks and stubbornly set jaw. His thickly lashed eyes were the same deep, espresso coffee brown, so dark she could not make out his pupils or his mood.

He rose to his feet, but whether it was out of politeness or a desire to intimidate Natalie wasn't quite sure. At six foot four he was impressively, imposingly tall. Even in heels she had to crane her neck to maintain eye contact.

She sent the tip of her tongue out to moisten her

concrete-dry lips. She had to keep her cool. She had spent most of her life keeping her emotions under the strictest control. Now was not the time to show how worried she was about the situation with her brother. Angelo would feed off that and work it to his advantage. All she had to do was pay for the damage Lachlan had caused, then get out of here and never look back.

'Thank you for seeing me at short notice,' she said. 'I understand how busy you are. I won't take up too much of your time.'

Those incredibly dark, inscrutable eyes nailed hers relentlessly as he reached across to press the intercom. 'Fiona, postpone my engagements for the next hour,' he said. 'And hold all my calls. On no account am I to be interrupted.'

'Will do.'

Natalie blinked at him as he straightened. 'Look, there's really no need to interrupt your busy schedule—'

'There is every need,' he said, still holding her gaze with the force of his. 'What your brother did to one of my hotel rooms in Rome is a criminal offence.'

'Yes,' she said, swallowing again. 'I know. But he's been going through a difficult stage just now, and I—'

One of his jet-black brows lifted satirically. 'What "difficult stage" would that be?' he asked. 'Has Daddy taken away his Porsche or cut back his allowance?'

She pressed her lips together, summoning control over emotions that were threatening to spill over. How dared Angelo mock what her brother had to deal with? Lachlan was a ticking time bomb. It was up to her to stop him from self-destructing. She hadn't been able to save her baby brother all those years ago, but she would move heaven and earth to get it right this time with Lachlan.

'He's just a kid,' she began. 'He's only just left school and—'

'He's eighteen,' Angelo said through tight, angry lips. 'He's old enough to vote and in my opinion old enough to face up to the consequences of his actions. He and his drunken friends have caused over a hundred thousand pounds' worth of damage to one of my most prestigious hotels.'

Natalie's stomach nosedived. *Was he exaggerating?* The way her mother had described it had made her think it hadn't been much more than the cost of a carpet-clean and the replacement of a few furnishings—perhaps a repaint on one of the walls.

What had Lachlan been thinking? What on earth had made him go on such a crazy rampage?

'I'm prepared to reimburse you for the damage, but before I hand over any money I'd like to see the damage for myself,' she said, with a jut of her chin.

His dark eyes challenged hers. 'So you're prepared to foot the bill personally, are you?'

She eyeballed him back, even though her stomach was churning at the menacing look in his eyes. 'Within reason.'

His top lip curled. 'You have no clue about what you're letting yourself in for,' he said. 'Do you have any idea what your brother gets up to when he's out night-clubbing with his friends?'

Natalie was all too aware, and for the last few months it had been keeping her awake at night. She knew why Lachlan was behaving the way he was, but there was little she could do to stop him. Lachlan had been the replacement child after Liam had died—the lost son re-incarnated. Since birth he had been forced to live not his own life but Liam's. All the hopes and dreams their parents had envisaged for Liam had been transferred to Lachlan, and lately he had started to buckle under the pressure. She was terrified that one day soon he would go, or be pushed too far.

She already had one death on her hands. She could not bear to have another.

'How do you know Lachlan is responsible for the damage?' she asked. 'How do you know it wasn't one of his friends?'

Angelo looked at her with dagger-sharp eyes. 'The room was booked in his name,' he said. 'It was his credit card that was presented at check-in. He is legally responsible, even if he didn't so much as knock a cushion out of place.'

Natalie suspected her brother had done a whole lot more than rearrange a few sofa cushions. She had more than once witnessed him in the aftermath of one of his drinking binges. Lachlan wasn't a sleepy drunk or a happy, loquacious one. A few too many drinks unleashed a rage inside him that was as terrifying as it was sudden. And yet a few hours later he would have no memory of the things he had said and done.

So far he had managed to escape prosecution, but only because their rich and influential father had pulled in some favours with the authorities.

But that was here in Britain.

Right now Lachlan was at the mercy of the Italian authorities—which was why she had come to London to appeal to Angelo on his behalf. Of all the hotels in Rome, why had he stayed at one of Angelo Bellandini's?

Natalie opened her bag and took out her chequebook with a sigh of resignation. 'All right,' she said, hunting for a pen. 'I'll take your word for it and pay for the damage.'

Angelo barked out a sardonic laugh. 'You think after you scrawl your signature across that cheque I'll simply overlook this?' he asked.

She quickly disguised another swallow. 'You want more than one hundred thousand pounds?' she asked, in a voice that sounded too high—squeaky, almost.

He looked at her, his eyes meshing with hers in a lockdown that made the silence throb with palpable tension. She felt it moving up her spine, vertebrae by vertebrae. She felt it on her skin, in the ghosting of goose bumps fluttering along her flesh. She felt it— shockingly—between her thighs, as if he had reached down and stroked her there with one of his long, clever fingers.

He didn't say a word. He didn't need to. She could read the subtext of that dark, mocking gaze. He didn't give a toss about the money. It wasn't money he wanted. He had more than enough of his own.

Natalie knew exactly what he wanted. She had known it the minute she had stepped into his office and locked gazes with him.

He wanted her.

'Take it or leave it,' she said, and slammed the cheque on the desk between them.

He picked up the cheque and slowly and deliberately tore it into pieces, then let them fall like confetti on the desk, all the while holding her gaze with the implacable and glittering force of his. 'As soon as you walk out of here I'll notify the authorities in Rome to press charges,' he said. 'Your brother will go to prison. I'll make sure of it.'

Natalie's heart banged against the wall of her chest like a pendulum slammed by a prize-fighter's punch. How long would her brother last in a foreign prison?

He would be housed amongst murderers and thieves and rapists. It could be *years* before a magistrate heard his case. He was just a kid. Yes, he had done wrong, but it wasn't his fault—not really. He needed help, not imprisonment.

'Why are you doing this?' she asked.

His mouth lifted in a half-smile, his eyes taunting hers with merciless intent. 'You can't guess, *mia piccola*?'

She drew in a painfully tight breath. 'Isn't this taking revenge a little too far? What happened between us *is* between us. It has nothing to do with my brother. It has nothing to do with anyone but us.' *With me*, she added silently. *It's always been to do with me*.

His eyes glinted dangerously and his smile completely vanished until his lips were just a thin line of contempt. 'Why did you do it?' he asked. 'Why did you leave me for a man you picked up in a bar like a trashy little two-bit hooker?'

Natalie couldn't hold his gaze. It wasn't a lie she was particularly proud of. But back then it had been the only way she could see of getting him to let her go. He had fallen in love with her. He had mentioned marriage and babies. He had already bought an engagement ring. She had come across it while putting his socks away. It had glinted at her with its diamond eye, taunting her, reminding her of all she wanted but could never have.

She had panicked.

'I wasn't in love with you.' That was at least the truth…sort of. She had taught herself not to love. Not to feel. Not to be at the mercy of emotions that could not be controlled.

If you loved you lost.

If you cared you got hurt.

If you opened your heart someone would rip it out of your chest when you least expected it.

The physical side of things…well, that had been different. She had let herself lose control. Not that she'd really had a choice. Angelo had seen to that. Her body had been under the mastery of his from the first time he had kissed her. She might have locked down her emotions, but her physical response to him still echoed in her body like the haunting melody of a tune she couldn't forget no matter how hard she tried.

'So it was just sex?' he said.

Natalie forced herself to meet his gaze, and then wished she hadn't when she saw the black hatred glittering there. 'I was only twenty-one,' she said, looking away again. 'I didn't know what I wanted back then.'

'Do you know now?'

She caught the inside of her mouth with her teeth. 'I know what I don't want,' she said.

'Which is?'

She met his gaze again. 'Can we get to the point?' she asked. 'I've come here to pay for the damage my brother allegedly caused. If you won't accept my money, then what will you accept?'

It was a dangerous question to be asking. She knew it as soon as she voiced it. It hung in the ensuing silence, mocking her, taunting her for her supposed immunity.

She had *never* been immune.

It had all been an act—a clever ploy to keep him from guessing how much she'd wanted to be free to love him. But the clanging chains of her past had kept her anchored in silence. She couldn't love him or anyone.

Angelo's diamond-hard gaze tethered hers. 'Why don't you sit down and we can discuss it?' he said, gesturing to a chair near to where she was standing.

Natalie sank into the chair with relief. Her legs were so shaky the ligaments in her legs felt as if they had been severed like the strings of a puppet. Her heart was pounding and her skin was hot and clammy in spite of the air conditioning. She watched as he went back to the other side of his desk and sat down. For someone so tall he moved with an elegant, loose-limbed grace. His figure was rangy and lean, rather than excessively gym-pumped, although there was nothing wrong with the shape of his biceps. She could see the firm outline of them beneath his crisp ice-blue shirt. The colour was a perfect foil for his olive-toned skin. In the past she had only ever seen him in casual clothes, or wearing nothing at all.

In designer business clothes he looked every inch the successful hotel and property tycoon—untouchable, remote, in control. Her hands and mouth had traced every slope and plane and contour of his body. She could still remember how salty his skin tasted against her tongue. She still remembered the scent of him, the musk and citrus blend that had clung to her skin for hours after their making love. She remembered the thrusting possession of his body, how his masterful touch had unlocked her tightly controlled responses like a maestro with a difficult instrument that no one else could play.

She gave herself a mental slap and sat up straighter in the chair. Crossing her legs and arms, she fixed her gaze on Angelo's with a steely composure she was nowhere near feeling.

He leaned back in his own chair, with his fingers steepled against his chin, his dark gaze trained with unnervingly sharp focus on hers. 'I've heard anybody who is anybody is sleeping between your sheets,' he said.

She returned his look with chilly hauteur. 'I don't suppose *you* are doing so.'

His lips gave a tiny twitch of amusement, his dark eyes smouldering as they continued to hold hers. 'Not yet,' he said.

Natalie's insides flickered with the memory of long-ago desire. She'd fought valiantly to suppress it, but from the moment she had stepped into his office she had been aware of her body and its unruly response to him. He had always had that power over her. Just a look, an idle touch, a simple word and she would melt.

She couldn't afford to give in to past longings. She had to be strong in order to get through this. Lachlan's future depended on her. If this latest misdemeanour of his got out in the tabloids his life would be ruined. He was hoping to go to Harvard after this gap year. A criminal record would ruin everything for him.

Their father would crucify him.

He would crucify them both.

Natalie blamed herself. Why hadn't she realised how disenfranchised Lachlan was? Had she somehow given him some clue to her past history with Angelo? Had her lack of an active love-life made him suspect Angelo was the cause? How had he put two and two together? It wasn't as if she had ever been one to wear her heart on her sleeve. She had been busy building up her business. She had not missed dating. She'd had one or two encounters that had left her cold. She had more or less decided she wasn't cut out for an intimate relationship. The passion she had experienced with Angelo had come at a huge price, and it wasn't one she was keen to pay again.

She was better off alone.

'I understand how incredibly annoyed you are at

what my brother has supposedly done,' she said. 'But I must beg you not to proceed with criminal charges.'

His dark brow lifted again. 'Let me get this straight,' he said. 'You're *begging* me?'

Natalie momentarily compressed her lips in an attempt to control her spiralling emotions. How like him to taunt her. He would milk this situation for all it was worth and she would have to go along with it. He knew it. She knew it. He wanted her pride. It would be his ultimate trophy.

'I'm asking for leniency.'

'You're grovelling.'

She straightened her shoulders again. 'I'm asking you to drop all charges,' she said. 'I'll cover the damages— even double, if you insist. You won't be out of pocket.'

His gaze still measured hers unwaveringly. 'You want this to go away before it gets out in the press, don't you?' he said.

Natalie hoped her expression wasn't giving away any sign of her inner panic. She had always prided herself on disguising her feelings. Years of dealing with her father's erratic mood swings had made her a master at concealing her fear in case it was exploited. From childhood her ice-cold exterior had belied the inner turmoil of her emotions. It was her shield, her armour—her carapace of protection.

But Angelo had a keen, intelligent gaze. Even before she had left him she had felt he was starting to sum up her character in a way she found incredibly unsettling.

'Of course I want to keep this out of the press,' she said. 'But then, don't you? What will people think of your hotel security if a guest can do the sort of damage you say my brother did? Your hotels aim for the top end of the market. What does that say about the type of clientele your hotel attracts?'

A muscle flickered like a pulse at the side of his mouth. 'I have reason to believe your brother specifically targeted my hotel,' he said.

She felt her stomach lurch. 'What makes you think that?'

He opened a drawer to the left of him and took out a sheet of paper and handed it to her across the desk. She took it with a hand that wasn't quite steady. It was a faxed copy of a note addressed to Angelo, written in her brother's writing. It said: *This is for my sister.*

Natalie gulped and handed back the paper. 'I don't know what to say... I have never said anything to Lachlan about...about us. He was only thirteen when we were together. He was at boarding school when we shared that flat in Notting Hill. He never even met you.'

Nor had any of her family. She hadn't wanted Angelo to be exposed to her father's outrageous bigotry and her mother's sickening subservience.

'You must have said something to him,' Angelo said. 'Why else would he write that?'

Natalie chewed at her lip. She had said nothing to anyone other than that her short, intense and passionate affair with Angelo was over because she wanted to concentrate on her career. Not even her closest girlfriend, Isabel Astonberry, knew how much her break-up with Angelo had affected her. She had told everyone she was suffering from anxiety. Even her doctor had believed her. It had explained the rapid weight loss and agitation and sleepless nights. She had almost convinced *herself* it was true. She had even taken the pills the doctor had prescribed, but they hadn't done much more than throw a thick blanket over her senses, numbing her until she felt like a zombie.

Eventually she had climbed out of the abyss of misery and got on with her life. Hard work had been her remedy. It still was. Her interior design business had taken off soon after she had qualified. Her online sales were expanding exponentially, and she had plans to set up some outlets in Europe. She employed staff who managed the business end of things while she got on with what she loved best—the designing of her linen and soft furnishings range.

And she had done it all by herself. She hadn't used her father's wealth and status to recruit clients. Just like Angelo, she had been adamant that she would not rely on family wealth and privilege, but do it all on her own talent and hard work.

'Natalie?' Angelo's deep voice jolted her out of her reverie. 'Why do you think your brother addressed that note to me?'

She averted her gaze as she tucked a strand of hair behind her ear. 'I don't know.'

'He must have known it would cause immense trouble for you,' he said.

Natalie looked up at him again, her heart leaping to her throat. 'A hundred thousand pounds is a lot of money, but it's not a lot to pay for someone's freedom,' she said.

He gave an enigmatic half-smile. 'Ah, yes, but whose freedom are we talking about?'

A ripple of panic moved through her as she held his unreadable gaze. 'Can we quit it with the game-playing?' she said. 'Why don't you come straight out and say what you've planned in terms of retribution?'

His dark eyes hardened like black ice. 'I think you

know what I want,' he said. 'It's the same thing I wanted five years ago.'

She drew in a sharp little breath. 'You can't possibly want an affair with someone you hate. That's so... so cold-blooded.'

He gave a disaffected smile. 'Who said anything about an affair?'

She felt a fine layer of sweat break out above her top lip. She felt clammy and light-headed. Her legs trembled even though she had clamped them together to hide it. She unclenched her hands and put one to her throat, where her heart seemed to have lodged itself like a pigeon trapped in a narrow pipe.

'You're joking, of course,' she said, in a voice that was hoarse to the point of barely being audible.

Those dark, inscrutable eyes held hers captive, making every nerve in her body acutely aware of his sensual power over her. Erotic memories of their past relationship simmered in the silence. Every passionate encounter, from their first kiss to their blistering bloodletting last, hovered in the tense atmosphere. She felt the incendiary heat and fire of his touch just by looking at him. It was all she could do to stay still and rigidly composed in her chair.

'I want a wife,' he said, as if stating his desire for something as prosaic as a cup of tea or coffee.

Natalie hoisted her chin. 'Then I suggest you go about the usual way of acquiring one,' she said.

'I tried that and it didn't work,' he returned. 'I thought I'd try this way instead.'

She threw him a scathing look. 'Blackmail, you mean?'

He gave an indifferent shrug of one of his broad shoulders. 'Your brother will likely spend up to four years waiting for a hearing,' he said. 'The legal system in Italy is expensive and time consuming. I don't need to tell you he is unlikely to escape conviction. I have enough proof to put him away for a decade.'

Natalie shot to her feet, her control slipping like a stiletto on a slick of oil. 'You bastard!' she said. 'You're only doing this to get at me. Why don't you admit it? You only want revenge because I am the first woman who has ever left you. That's what this is about, isn't it? Your damned pride got bruised, so now you're after revenge.'

His jaw locked down like a clamp, his lips barely moving as he commanded, 'Sit down.'

She glared at him with undiluted hatred. 'Go to hell.'

He placed his hands on the desk and slowly got to his feet. Somehow it was far more threatening than if he had shoved his chair back with aggressive force. His expression was thunderous, but when he spoke it was with icy calm.

'We will marry as soon as I can get a licence. If you do not agree, then your brother will face the consequences of his actions. Do you have anything to say?'

She said it in unladylike coarseness. The crude words rang in the air, but rather than make her feel powerful they made her feel ashamed. He had made her lose control and she hated him for it.

Angelo's top lip slanted in a mocking smile. 'I am not averse to the odd moment of self-pleasuring, as you so charmingly suggest, but I would much rather share the experience with a partner. And, to be quite frank, no one does it better than you.'

She snatched up her bag and clutched it against her body so tightly she felt the gold pen inside jab her in the stomach. 'I hope you die and rot in hell,' she said.

'I hope you get some horrible, excruciatingly painful pestilent disease and suffer tortuous agony for the rest of your days.'

He continued to stare her down with irritatingly cool calm. 'I love you too, Tatty,' he said.

Natalie felt completely and utterly ambushed by the use of his pet name for her. It was like a body-blow to hear it after all these years. Her chest gave an aching spasm. Her anger dissolved like an aspirin in a glass of water. Her fighting spirit collapsed like a warrior stung by a poison dart. Tears sprang at the back of her eyes. She could feel them burning and knew if she didn't get out of there right now he would see them.

She spun around and groped blindly for the door, somehow getting it open and stumbling through it, leaving it open behind her like a mouth in the middle of an unfinished sentence.

She didn't bother with the lift.

She didn't even glance at the receptionist on her way to the fire escape.

She bolted down the stairs as if the devil and all his maniacal minions were on her heels.

CHAPTER TWO

NATALIE got back to her hotel and leant against the closed door of her suite with her chest still heaving like a pair of bellows. The ringing of her phone made her jump, and she almost dropped it when she tried to press the answer button with fingers that felt like cotton wool.

'H-hello?'

'Natalie, it's me...Lachlan.'

She pushed herself away from the door and scraped a hand through her sticky hair as she paced the floor in agitation. 'I've been trying to call you for the last twenty-four hours!' she said. 'Where are you? What's going on? Why did you do it? For God's sake, Lachlan, are you out of your mind?'

'I'm sorry,' he said. 'Look, I'm only allowed one call. I'll have to make it quick.'

Natalie scrunched her eyes closed, not wanting to picture the ghastly cell he would be locked in, with vicious-looking prison guards watching his every move. 'Tell me what to do,' she said, opening her eyes again to look at the view of the River Thames and the London Eye. 'Tell me what you need. I'll get there as soon as I can.'

'Just do what Angelo tells you to do,' Lachlan said. 'He's got it all under control. He can make this go away.'

She swung away from the window. *'Are you nuts?'* she said.

He released a sigh. 'He'll do the right thing by you, Nat,' he said. 'Just do whatever he says.'

She started pacing again—faster this time. 'He wants to marry me,' she said. 'Did he happen to mention that little detail to you?'

'You could do a whole lot worse.'

Her mouth dropped open. 'Lachlan, you're surely not serious? He *hates* me.'

'He's my only chance,' he said. 'I know I've stuffed up. I don't want to go to prison. Angelo's given me a choice. I have to take it.'

She gave a disgusted snort. 'He's given *me* a choice, not you,' she said. 'My freedom in exchange for yours.'

'It doesn't have to be for ever,' he said. 'You can divorce him after a few months. He can't force you to stay with him indefinitely.'

Natalie seriously wondered about that. Rich, powerful men were particularly adept at getting and keeping what they wanted. Look at their father, for instance. He had kept their mother chained to his side in spite of years of his infidelities and emotional cruelty. She could not bear to end up in the same situation as her mother. A trophy wife, a pretty adornment, a plaything that could be picked up and put down at will. With no power of her own other than a beauty that would one day fade, leaving her with nothing but diamonds, designer clothes and drink to compensate for her loneliness.

'Why did you do it?' she asked. 'Why his hotel?'

'Remember the last time we caught up?' Lachlan said.

Natalie remembered all too well. It had been a weekend in Paris a couple of months ago, when she had been attending a fabric show. Lachlan had been at a friend's eighteenth birthday party just outside of the city. He had been ignominiously tossed out of his friend's parents' château after disgracing himself after a heavy night of drinking.

'Yes,' she said in stern reproach. 'It took me weeks to get the smell of alcohol and vomit out of my coat.'

'Yeah, well, I saw that gossip magazine open on the passenger seat,' he said. 'There was an article about Angelo and his latest lover. That twenty-one-year-old heiress from Texas?'

She tried to ignore the dagger of jealousy that spiked her when she recalled the article, and the stunningly gorgeous young woman who had been draped on Angelo's arm at some highbrow function.

'So,' she said. 'What of it? It wasn't the first time he'd squired some brainless little big-boobed bimbo to an event.'

'No,' Lachlan said. 'But it was the first time I'd seen you visibly upset by it.'

'I wasn't upset,' she countered quickly. 'I was disgusted.'

'Same difference.'

Natalie blew out a breath and started pacing again. 'So you took it upon yourself to get back at him by trashing one of the most luxurious hotel rooms in the whole of Europe just because you thought I was a little peeved?'

'I know, I know, I know,' Lachlan said. 'It sounds so stupid now. I'm not sure why I did it. I guess I was just angry that he seemed to have it all together and you didn't.'

Natalie frowned. 'What do you mean?' she said. 'I'm

running a successful business all by myself. I'm paying for my own home. I'm happy with my life.'

'Are you, Nat?' he asked. 'Are you really?'

The silence was condemning.

'You work ridiculous hours,' Lachlan went on. 'You never take holidays.'

'I hate flying, that's why.'

'You could do a desensitising programme for that,' he said.

'I don't have time.'

'It's because of what happened to Liam, isn't it?' Lachlan said. 'You haven't been on a plane since he drowned in Spain all those years ago.'

Natalie felt the claws of guilt clutch her by the throat. She still remembered the tiny white coffin with her baby brother's body in it being loaded on the tarmac. She had seen it from her window seat. She had sat there staring at it, with an empty, aching, hollow feeling in her chest.

It had been her fault he had been found floating face-down in that pool.

'I have to go,' Lachlan said. 'I'm being transferred.'

Her attention snapped back to Lachlan's dire situation. 'Transferred where?' she asked.

'Just do what Angelo says, please?' he said. 'Nat, I need you to do what he wants. He's promised to keep this out of the press. I have to accept his help. My life is over if I don't. Please?'

Natalie pinched the bridge of her nose until her eyes smarted with bitter angry tears. The cage of her conscience came down with a snap.

She was trapped.

* * *

Angelo was finalising some details on a project in Malaysia when his receptionist announced he had a visitor. 'It's Natalie Armitage,' Fiona said.

He leaned back in his chair and smiled a victor's smile. He had waited a long time for this opportunity. He wanted her to beg, to plead and to grovel. It was payback time for the misery she had put him through by walking out on him so heartlessly.

'Tell her to wait,' he said. 'I have half an hour of paperwork to get through that can't be put off.'

There was a quick muffled exchange of words and Fiona came back on the intercom. 'Miss Armitage said she's not going to wait. She said if you don't see her now she is going to get back on the train to Edinburgh and you'll never see her again.'

Angelo slowly drummed his fingers on the desk. He was used to Natalie's obstinacy. She was a stubborn, headstrong little thing. Her independence had been one of the first things he had admired about her, and yet in the end it had been the thing that had frustrated him the most. She'd absolutely refused to bend to his will. She'd stood up to him as no one else had ever dared.

He was used to people doing as he said. From a very young age he had given orders and people had obeyed them. It was part of the territory. Coming from enormous wealth, you had power. You had privilege and people respected that.

But not his little Tatty.

He leaned forward and pressed the button. 'Tell her I'll see her in fifteen minutes.'

He had not even sat back in his chair when the door slammed open and Natalie came storming in. Her brown hair with its natural highlights was in disarray about her flushed-with-fury face. Her hands were clenched into combative fists by her sides, and her slate-blue eyes were flashing like the heart of a gas flame. He could see the outline of her beautiful breasts as they rose and fell beneath her top.

His groin tightened and jammed with lust.

'You…you *bastard*!' she said.

Angelo rocked back in his chair. *'Cara,'* he said. 'I'm absolutely delighted to see you, too. How long has it been? Four hours?'

She glowered at him. 'Where have you taken him?'

He elevated one brow. 'Where have I taken whom?'

Her eyes narrowed to needle-thin slits. 'My brother,' she said. 'I can't contact him. He's not answering his phone any more. How do I know you're doing the right thing by him?'

'Your brother is in good hands,' he said. 'That is as long as you do what is required.'

Her eyes blazed with venomous hatred. 'How can I trust you to uphold your side of the bargain?' she asked.

'You can trust me, Natalie.'

She made a scoffing sound. 'I'd rather take my chances with a death adder.'

Angelo smiled a thin-lipped smile. 'I'm afraid a death adder is not going to hold any sway with an Italian magistrate,' he said. 'I can get your brother out of harm's way with the scrawl of my signature.' He picked up a pen for effect. 'What's it going to be?'

He saw her eyes go to his pen. He saw the way her jaw locked as she clenched her teeth. Her saw the way her slim throat rose and fell. He saw the battle on her face as her will locked horns with his. He felt the energy of her anger like a high-voltage current in the air.

'You can't force me to sleep with you,' she bit out.

'You might be able to force me to wear your stupid ring, but you can't force me to do anything else.'

'You will be my wife in every sense of the word,' he said. 'In public and in private. Otherwise the deal is off.'

Her jaw worked some more. He could even hear her teeth grinding together. Her eyes were like twin blasts from a roaring furnace.

'I didn't think you could ever go so low as this,' she said. 'You can have anyone you want. You have women queuing up to be with you. Why on earth do you want an unwilling wife? Is this some sort of sick obsession? What can you possibly hope to achieve out of this?'

Angelo slowly swung his ergonomic chair from side to side as he surveyed her outraged features. 'I quite fancy the idea of taming you,' he said. 'You're like a beautiful wild brumby that bucks and kicks and bites because it doesn't want anyone to get too close.'

Her cheeks flushed a fiery red and her eyes kept on shooting sparks of ire at him. 'So you thought you'd slip a lasso around my neck and whip me into submission, did you?' she said, with a curl of her bee-stung top lip. 'Good luck with that.'

Angelo smiled a lazy smile. 'You know me, Tatty. I just love a challenge—and the bigger the better.'

Her brows shot together in a furious frown. 'Don't call me that.'

'Why not?' he said. 'I always used to call you that.'

She stalked to the other side of the room, her arms across her body in a keep-away-from-me pose. 'I don't want you to call me that now,' she said, her gaze determinedly averted from his.

'I will call you what I damn well want,' he said, feeling his anger and frustration rising. 'Look at me.'

She gave her head a toss and kept her eyes fixed on the painting on the wall. 'Go to hell.'

Angelo got to his feet and walked over to where she was standing. He put a hand on her shoulder, but she spun around and slapped at his hand as if it was a nasty insect.

'Don't you *dare* touch me,' she snarled at him, like a wildcat.

He felt the fizzing of his fingers where his hand had briefly come into contact with her slim shoulder. The sensation travelled all the way to his groin. He looked at her mouth—that gorgeous, full-lipped mouth that had kissed him with such passion and fire in the past. He had felt those soft lips around him, drawing the essence from him until he had been legless with ecstasy. She had lit fires of need over his whole body with her hot little tongue. Her fingers had danced over every inch of his flesh, caressing and stroking him, branding him with the memory of her touch.

Ever since she had left him he had waited for this moment—for a chance to prove to her how much she wanted him in spite of her protestations. His rage at being cut from her life had festered inside him. It had soured every other relationship since. He could not seem to find what he was looking for with anyone else. He had gone from relationship to relationship, some lasting only a date or two, none of them lasting more than a month. Lately he had even started to wonder if he had imagined how perfectly physically in tune he had been with her. But seeing her again, being in the same room as her, sensing her reaction to him and his to her, proved to him it wasn't his imagination.

She wouldn't be the one who walked out on him without notice this time around. She would stay with him until he decided he'd had enough. It might take a month or two, maybe even up to a year, but he would not give her the chance to rip his heart open again. He would not allow her that close again. He had been a passionate fool five years ago. From the moment he had met her he had fallen—and fallen hard. He had envisaged their future together, how they would build on the empire of his grandparents and parents, how they would be the next generation of Bellandinis.

But then she had ripped the rug from under his feet by betraying him.

She might hate him for what he was doing, but right now he didn't give a damn. He wanted her and he was going to have her. She would come to him willingly. He would make sure of that. There would be no forcing, no coercing. Behind that ice-maiden façade was a fiercely passionate young woman. He had unleashed that passion five years ago and he would do so again.

'In time you will be begging for my touch, *cara*,' he said. 'Just like you did in the past.'

Her expression shot more daggers at him. 'Can't you see how much I hate you?' she said.

'I can see passion, not hate,' he said. 'That is promising, *si*?'

She let out a breath and put more distance between them, her look guarded and defensive. 'How soon do you expect to get this ridiculous plan of yours off the ground?' she asked.

'We will marry at the end of next week,' he said. 'There's no point dilly-dallying.'

'Next week?' she asked, eyes widening. 'Why so soon?'

Angelo held her gaze. 'I know how your mind works, Natalie. I'm not leaving anything up to chance. The sooner we are married, the sooner your brother gets out of trouble.'

'Can I see him?'

'No.'

She frowned. 'Why not?'

'He's not allowed visitors,' Angelo said.

'But that's ridiculous!' she said. 'Of course he's allowed visitors. It's a basic human right.'

'Not where he is currently staying,' he said. 'You'll see him soon enough. In the meantime, I think it's time I met the rest of your family—don't you agree?'

Something shifted behind her gaze. 'Why do you want to meet my family?' she said. 'Anyway, apart from Lachlan there is only my parents.'

'Most married couples meet their respective families,' Angelo said. 'My parents will want to meet you. And my grandparents and uncles and aunts and cousins.'

She gave him a worried look. 'They're not all coming to the ceremony, are they?'

'But of course,' he said. 'We will fly to Rome on Tuesday. The wedding will be on Saturday, at my grandparents' villa, in the private chapel that was built especially for their wedding day sixty years ago.'

Her eyes looked like a startled fawn's. 'F-fly?'

'*Si, cara,*' he said dryly. 'On an aeroplane. You know—those big things that take off at the airport and take you where you want to go? I have a private one—a Lear jet that my family use to get around.'

Her mouth flattened obstinately. 'I'm not flying.'

Angelo frowned. 'What do you mean, you're not flying?'

She shifted her gaze, her arms tightening across her body. 'I'm *not* flying.'

It took Angelo a moment or two to figure it out. It shocked him that he hadn't picked it up before. It all made sense now that he thought about it.

'That's why you caught the train down from Edinburgh yesterday,' he said. 'That's why, when I suggested five years ago that we take that cut-price trip to Malta, you said you couldn't afford it and refused to let me pay for you. We had a huge fight over it. You wouldn't speak to me for days. It wasn't about your independence, was it? You're frightened of flying.'

She turned her back on him and stood looking out of his office window, the set of her spine as rigid as a plank. 'Go on,' she said. 'Call me a nut job. You wouldn't be the first.'

Angelo released a long breath. 'Natalie… Why didn't you tell me?'

She still stood looking out of the window with her back to him. '*Hi, my name's Natalie Armitage and I'm terrified of flying.* Yeah, that would have really got your notice that night in the bar.'

'What got my notice in that bar was your incredible eyes,' he said. 'And the fact that you stood up to that creep who was trying it on with you.'

He saw the slight softening of her spine and shoulders, as if the memory of that night had touched something deep inside her, unravelling one of the tight cords of resolve she had knotted in place. 'You didn't have to rescue me like some big macho caveman,' she said after a short pause. 'I could've taken care of it myself.'

'I was brought up to respect and protect women,' Angelo said. 'That guy was a drunken fool. I enjoyed hauling him out to the street. He was lucky I didn't rearrange his teeth for him. God knows I was tempted.'

She turned and looked at him, her expression still

intractable. 'I don't want to fly, Angelo,' she said. 'It's easy enough to drive. It'll only take a couple of days. I'll make my own way there if you can't spare the time.'

Angelo studied her dark blue gaze. He saw the usual obstinacy glittering there, but behind that was a flicker of fear—like a stagehand peeping out from behind the curtains to check on the audience. It made him wonder if he had truly known her five years ago. He had thought he had her all figured out, but this was a facet to her personality he had never even suspected. He had always prided himself on his perspicuity, on his ability to read people and situations. But he could see now that reading Natalie was like reading a complex multi-layered book.

'I'll be with you the whole time,' he said. 'I won't let anything happen to you.'

'That's hardly reassuring,' she said with a cynical look, 'considering this whole marriage thing you've set up is a plot for revenge.'

'My intention is not for you to suffer,' he said.

Her chin came up and her eyes flashed again. 'Oh, really?'

Angelo drew in a breath and released it forcefully as he went back behind his desk. He gripped the back of his chair as he faced her. 'Why must you search for nefarious motives in everything I do or say?'

She gave a little scoffing laugh. 'Pardon me for being a little suspicious, but you're surely not going to tell me you still care about me after all this time?'

Angelo's fingers dug deeper into the leather of his chair until his knuckles whitened. He didn't love her. He *refused* to love her. She had betrayed him. He was not going to forgive and forget that in a hurry. But he would *have* her. That was different. That had nothing to do with emotions.

He deliberately relaxed his grasp and sat down. 'We have unfinished business,' he said. 'I knew that the minute you walked in that door yesterday.'

'You're imagining things,' she said.

He put up one brow. 'Am I?'

She held his gaze for a beat, before she lowered it to focus on the glass paperweight on his desk. 'How long do you think this marriage will last?' she asked.

'It can last as long as we want it to,' Angelo said.

Her gaze met his again. 'Don't you mean as long as *you* want it to?' she asked.

He gave a little up and down movement of his right shoulder. 'You ended things the last time,' he said. 'Isn't it fair that I be the one to do so this time around?'

Her mouth tightened. 'I ended things because it was time to move on,' she said. 'We were fighting all the time. It wasn't a love match. It was a battlefield.'

'Oh, come *on*,' Angelo said. 'What are you talking about, Natalie? All couples fight. It's part and parcel of being in a relationship. There are always little power struggles. It's what makes life interesting.'

'That might have been the way you were brought up, but it certainly wasn't the way I was,' she said.

He studied her expression again, noting all the little nuances of her face: the way she chewed at the inside of her mouth but tried to hide it, the way her eyes flickered away from his but then kept tracking back, as if they were being pulled by a magnetic force, and the way her finely boned jaw tightened when she was feeling cornered.

'How *were* you brought up to resolve conflict?' he asked.

She reached for her bag and got to her feet. 'Look, I have a train to catch,' she said. 'I have a hundred and one things to see to.'

'Why didn't you drive down from Edinburgh?' he asked. 'You haven't suddenly developed a fear of driving too, have you?'

Her eyes hardened resentfully. 'No,' she said. 'I like travelling by train. I can read or sketch or listen to music. I find driving requires too much concentration— especially in a city as crowded as London. Besides, it's better for the environment. I want to reduce my carbon footprint.'

Angelo rose to his feet and joined her at the door, placing his hand on the doorknob to stop her escaping. 'I'll need you to sign some papers in the next day or two.'

Her chin came up. The hard glitter was back in her gaze. 'A prenuptial agreement?'

He glanced at her mouth. He ached to feel it move under the pressure of his. He could feel the surge of his blood filling him with urgent, ferocious need.

'Yes,' he said, meeting her gaze again. 'Do you have a problem with that?'

'No,' she said, eyeballing him right back. 'I'll have one of my own drawn up. I'm not letting you take away everything I've worked so hard for.'

He smiled and tapped her gently on the end of her nose. 'Touché,' he said.

She blinked at him, looking flustered and disorientated. 'I—I have to go,' she said, and made a grab for the doorknob.

Angelo captured her hand within his. Her small, delicate fingers were dwarfed by the thickness and length and strength of his. He watched her eyes widen as he slowly brought her hand up to his mouth. He stopped before making contact with his lips, just a hair's breadth from touching. He watched as her throat rose and fell. He felt the jerky little gust of her cinnamon-scented breath. He saw her glance at his mouth, saw too the quick nervous dart of her tongue as she swept it out over her lips.

'I'll be in touch,' he said, dropping her hand and opening the door for her. *'Ciao.'*

She brushed past him in the doorway and without a single word of farewell she left.

CHAPTER THREE

'CONGRATULATIONS,' said Linda, Natalie's assistant, the following morning when she arrived at work.

'Pardon?'

Linda held up a newspaper. 'Talk about keeping your cards close to your chest,' she said. 'I didn't even know you were dating anyone.'

'I'm…' Natalie took the paper and quickly scanned it. There was a short paragraph about Angelo and her and their upcoming nuptials. Angelo was quoted as saying he was thrilled they were back together and how much he was looking forward to being married next week.

'Is it true or is it a prank?' Linda asked.

Natalie put the paper down on the counter. 'It's true,' she said, chewing at her bottom lip.

'Pardon me if I'm overstepping the mark here, but you don't look too happy about it,' Linda said.

Natalie forced a smile to her face. 'Sorry, it's just been such a pain…er…keeping it quiet until now,' she said, improvising as she went. 'We didn't want anyone to speculate about us getting back together until we were sure it was what we both wanted.'

'Gosh, how romantic!' Linda said. 'A secret relationship.'

'Not so secret now,' Natalie said a little ruefully as

her stomach tied itself in knots. How was she going to cope with the constant press attention? They would swarm about her like bees. Angelo was used to being chased by the paparazzi. He was used to cameras flashing in his face and articles being written that were neither true nor false but somewhere in between.

She liked her privacy. She guarded it fiercely. Now she would be thrust into the public arena not for her designs and her talent but for whom she was sleeping with.

Her stomach gave another little shuffle. Not that she would be actually sleeping with Angelo. She was determined not to give in to that particular temptation. Her body might still have some sort of programmed response to him, but that didn't mean she had to give in to it.

She could be strong.

She *would* be strong.

And determined.

He wouldn't find her so easy to seduce this time around. She had been young and relatively inexperienced five years ago. She was older and wiser now. She hadn't fallen in love with him before and she wasn't about to fall in love with him now. He would be glad to call an end to their marriage before a month or two. She couldn't see him tolerating her intransigence for very long. He was used to getting his own way. He wanted a submissive, I'll-do-anything-to-please-you wife.

There wasn't a bone in Natalie's body that would bend to any man's will, and certainly not to Angelo Bellandini's.

'These came for you while you were at the lawyer's,' Linda said when Natalie came back to the studio a couple of hours later.

Natalie looked at the massive bunch of blood-red roses elegantly wrapped and ribboned, their intoxicating clove-like perfume filling the air.

'Aren't you going to read the card?' Linda asked.

'Er…yes,' Natalie said unpinning the envelope from the cellophane and tissue wrap. She took the card out and read: *See you tonight, Angelo.*

'From Angelo?' Linda asked.

'Yes,' Natalie said, frowning.

'What's wrong?'

'Nothing.'

'You're frowning.'

She quickly relaxed her features. 'I've got a few things to see to in my office at home. Do you mind holding the fort here for the rest of the day?'

'Not at all,' Linda said. 'I guess you'll have to leave me in charge when you go on your honeymoon, right?'

Natalie gave her a tight on-off smile as she grabbed her bag and put the strap over her shoulder. 'I don't think I'll be away very long,' she said.

'Aren't you going to take the roses with you?' Linda asked.

Natalie turned back and scooped them up off the counter. 'Good idea,' she said, and left.

Angelo looked at the three-storey house in a leafy street in the well-to-do Edinburgh suburb of Morningside. It had a gracious elegance about it that reminded him of Natalie immediately. Even the garden seemed to reflect parts of her personality. The neatly clipped hedges and the meticulous attention to detail in plants and their colour and placement bore witness to a young woman who liked order and control.

He smiled to himself as he thought how annoyed she

would be at the way things were now *out* of her control. He had the upper hand and he was going to keep it. He would enjoy watching her squirm. He had five years of bitterness to avenge. Five years of hating her, five years of wanting her, five years of being tortured by memories of her body in his arms.

Five years of trying to replace her.

He put his finger to the highly polished brass doorbell. A chime-like sound rang out, and within a few seconds he heard the click-clack of her heels as she came to answer its summons. He could tell she was angry. He braced himself for the blast.

'How dare you release something to the press without checking with me first?' she said as her opening gambit.

'Hello, *cara*,' he said. 'I'm fine, thank you. And you?'

She glowered at him as she all but slammed the door once he had stepped over its threshold. 'You had no right to say anything to anyone,' she said. 'I was followed home by paparazzi. I had cameras going off in my face as soon as I left my studio. I almost got my teeth knocked out by one of their microphones.'

'Sorry about that,' he said. 'I'm so used to it I hardly notice it any more. Do you want me to get you a bodyguard? I should've thought of it earlier.'

She rolled her eyes. 'Of course I don't want a bloody bodyguard!' she said. 'I just want this to go away. I want *all* of this to go away.'

'It's not going to go away, Natalie,' he said. 'I'm not going to go away.'

She continued to glare at him. 'Why are you here?'

'I'm here to take you out to dinner.'

'What if I'm not hungry?'

'Then you can sit and watch me eat,' he said. 'Won't that be fun?'

'You are totally sick—do you know that?' she said.

'Did you like the roses?'

She turned away from him and began stalking down the wide corridor. 'I hate hothouse flowers,' she said. 'They have no scent.'

'I didn't buy you hothouse flowers,' he said. 'I had those roses shipped in from a private gardener.'

She gave a dismissive grunt and pushed open a door leading to a large formal sitting room. Again the attention to detail was stunning. Beautifully co-ordinated colours and luxurious fabrics, plush sofas and crystal chandeliers. Timeless antiques cleverly teamed with modern pieces—old-world charm and modern chic that somehow worked together brilliantly.

'Do you want a drink?' she asked uncharitably.

'What are you having?'

She threw him a speaking glance. 'I was thinking along the lines of cyanide,' she said.

He laughed. 'Not quite to my taste, *mia piccola*,' he said. 'Can I have a soda and lime?'

She went to a bar fridge that was hidden behind an art deco cabinet. He heard the rattle of ice cubes and the fizz of the soda water and then the plop of a slice of lime. She fixed her own glass of white wine before she turned and passed his drink to him with a combative look on her face.

'I hope it chokes you,' she said.

He lifted the glass against hers in a salute and said, 'To a long and happy marriage.'

Her gaze wrestled with his. 'I'm not drinking to that.'

'What will you drink to?'

She clanged her glass against his. 'To freedom,' she said, and took a sip.

Angelo watched her as she moved across the room,

her body movements stiff and unfriendly. She took another couple of sips of her drink, grimacing distastefully as if she wasn't used to drinking alcohol. 'I drove past your studio on the way here,' he said. 'Very impressive.'

She gave him a quick off-hand glance over her shoulder. 'Thank you.'

'I have a project for you, if you're interested,' he said.

She turned and looked at him fully. 'What sort of project?'

'A big one,' he said. 'It's worth a lot of money. Good exposure for you, too. It will bring you contacts from all over Europe.'

She stood very still before him, barely moving a muscle apart from the little hammer beat of tension at the base of her throat. 'Go on,' she said, with that same look of wariness in her gaze.

'I have a holiday villa in Sorrento, on the Amalfi Coast,' he said. 'I bought another property nearby for a song a few months back. I'm turning it into a luxury hotel. I'm just about done with the structural repairs. Now it's time for the interior makeover. I thought it would be a good project for you to take on once we are married.'

'Why do you want me to do it?' she asked.

'You're good at what you do,' he said.

Her mouth thinned in cynicism. 'And you want a carrot to dangle in front of me in case I happen to find a last-minute escape route?'

'You won't find an escape route,' he said. 'If you're a good girl I might even consider using your linen exclusively in all of my hotels. But only if you behave yourself.'

The look she gave him glittered with hatred. 'You've

certainly got blackmail down to a science,' she said. 'I didn't realise you were this ruthless five years ago.'

'I wasn't,' he said, taking another leisurely sip of his drink.

She tightened her mouth. 'I'll have to think about it,' she said. 'I have a lot of work on just now.'

'How capable is your assistant?' Angelo asked.

'Very capable,' she said. 'I'm thinking of promoting her. I need someone to handle the international end of things.'

'It must be quite limiting, not being able to do the travelling yourself,' he said.

She lifted a shoulder in a dismissive manner. 'I manage.'

Angelo picked up a small photo frame from an intricately carved drum table next to where he was standing. 'Is this Lachlan as a toddler?' he asked.

Her deep blue gaze flickered with something as she glanced at the photo. 'No,' she said. 'It's not.'

Angelo put the frame back on the table and, pushing back his sleeve, glanced at his watch. 'We should get going,' he said. 'I've booked the restaurant for eight.'

'I told you I'm not having dinner with you,' she said.

'And I told you to behave yourself,' he tossed back. 'You will join me for dinner and you will look happy about it. I don't care how you act in private, but in public you will at all times act like a young woman who is deeply in love. If you put even one toe of one foot out of line your brother will pay the price.'

She glared at him, her whole body bristling with anger. 'I've never been in love before, so how am I going to pull that act off with any authenticity?' she asked.

Angelo gave her a steely look. 'Make it up as you

go along,' he said, and put his glass down with a dull thud next to the photo frame. 'I'll be waiting outside in the car.'

Natalie waited until he had left the room before she picked up his glass. She mopped up the circle of condensation left on the leather top of the table with the heel of her hand and then wiped her hand against her churning stomach.

Her eyes went to the photo of Liam. He was standing on the beach with a bucket and spade in his dimpled hands, his cherubic face smiling for the camera. It had been taken just hours before he died. She remembered how excited he had been about the shells he had found. She remembered the sandcastle they had built together. She remembered how they had come back to the pool with their parents to rinse off. She remembered how her mother had gone inside for a rest and her father had left her with Liam while he made an important phone call...

She gently straightened the photo frame with fingers that were not quite steady. And then, with a sigh that burned like a serrated knife inside her chest, she went to get ready for dinner.

The restaurant Angelo had booked was a popular one that attracted the rich and the famous. Natalie had been a couple of times before, but no one had taken much notice of her. This time everyone looked and pointed as she came into the restaurant under Angelo's escort. A couple of people even took photos with their phones.

She tried to ignore the feel of his hand at her back. It was barely touching her but it felt like a brand. She could feel the tensile strength of him in that feather-light touch. It was a heady reminder of the sensual power he had over her.

Still had over her.

The *maître d'* led them to a table and then bustled off to fetch drinks after he had handed them both menus.

She buried her head in the menu even though she had no appetite. The words were just a blur in front of her. She blinked and tried to focus. A week ago she wouldn't have dreamed it possible for her to be sitting with Angelo in a restaurant. Ever since their break-up she had kept her distance both physically and mentally. But now she was back in his world and she wasn't sure how she was going to get out of it. How long would their marriage last, given the irreconcilable differences between them? He had loved her once, but he certainly wasn't motivated by love now. Revenge was his goal.

It had taken five years for the planets to align in his favour, but Lachlan had provided the perfect set-up for him to make her pay for leaving him. A man as proud and powerful as he was would not be satisfied until he had settled the score. How long would he insist on her staying with him? He surely wouldn't tie himself indefinitely to a loveless marriage. He was an only child. He was thirty-three years old—almost thirty-four. He would want children in the not too distant future. He would hardly want *her* to be the mother of his heirs. He would want someone biddable and obedient. Someone who would grace his many homes with poise and grace. Someone who wouldn't argue with him or question his opinions. Someone who would love him without reservation.

'Are you still a strict vegetarian?' Angelo asked.

Natalie looked at him over the top of the menu. 'I

occasionally eat chicken and fish,' she confessed a little sheepishly.

His dark brows lifted. 'You were so passionate back then.'

She lowered her gaze to the menu again. 'Yes, well, I was young and full of ideals back then. I've realised since that life is not so black and white.'

'What else have you changed your mind about?' he asked.

She put the menu to one side. 'I haven't changed that much,' she said.

'Meaning you still don't want children?'

Natalie felt the all too familiar pain seize her. She thought of Isabel's little newborn daughter Imogen, of how it had felt to hold her in her arms just a couple of weeks ago—the soft sweet smell, the tiny little starfish hands that had gripped hers so firmly. It had brought guilt down on her like a guillotine.

'No,' she said. 'I haven't changed my mind about that.'

'So you're still the high-powered career girl?' he said.

She picked up her glass and raised it in a salute. 'That's me.'

His dark brown eyes kept holding hers. 'What about when you're older?' he asked. 'You're young now, but what about when your biological clock starts to ramp up its ticking?'

'Not every woman is cut out to be a mother,' she said. 'I'm not good with kids. I think I must have missed out on the maternal gene.'

'I don't believe that,' he said. 'I accept that there are some women who genuinely don't want to have children, but you're a born nurturer. Look at the way you're prepared to put your neck on the line for your brother.'

She gave a careless shrug. 'I hate the thought of ruining my figure,' she said. 'I don't want stretch marks or sagging boobs.'

He made a sound at the back of his throat. 'For God's sake, Natalie, surely you're not that shallow?'

She met his gaze levelly. 'No, but I'm convinced some of your recent lovers have been.'

He gave her a glinting smile. 'So you've been keeping track of me over the years, have you, *cara*?' he asked.

'Not at all,' she said, looking away again. 'It is of no interest to me whatsoever who you sleep with. I have no hold over you. We dated. We broke up. That's it as far as I'm concerned.'

'We didn't just date,' he said. 'We lived together for five and a half months.'

Natalie picked up her drink, just for something to do with her hands. 'I only moved in with you because my flatmate's boyfriend moved in with us and made me feel I was in the way,' she said. 'Anyway, five months is not a long time compared to some relationships.'

'It was a long time for me.'

'Only because you've been playing musical beds since you were a teenager,' she said.

'Now who's talking?' he asked, with a diamond-hard glitter in his gaze as it clashed with hers.

Natalie wasn't ashamed of her past, but she wasn't proud of it either. While not exactly a constant bed-hopper, like some of her peers, she had occasionally used sex as a way to bolster her self-esteem. But the physical sensations had meant nothing to her until she had met Angelo. Not that she had ever told him. While she had been totally open with him physically, emotionally she had always held him slightly distant. She wondered if that was why he had found her so attractive. He was used to women falling head over heels in love with him and telling him so right from the start.

But she had not.

'Careful, Angelo,' she said. 'Your double standards are showing.'

His jaw tensed as he held her look. 'How long did you date the guy you replaced me with?' he asked.

'Not long,' she said.

'How long?'

'Is this really necessary?' she asked.

'I want to know.'

'We went out for a couple of weeks,' she said.

'Who broke it off?'

Natalie found his intent look unsettling. 'I did,' she said.

'So who have you dated since?'

'No one you would know,' she said. 'I try to keep my private life out of the papers.'

'Well done, you,' he said. 'I try to, but it's amazing how people find out stuff.'

'How do you stand it?' she asked.

He gave a little shrug. 'I'm used to it,' he said. 'My family's wealth has always kept us in the spotlight. The only time it cooled off a bit was when I came to study in London. I enjoyed being anonymous—not that it lasted long.'

'You lied to me.'

'I didn't lie to you,' he said. 'I just didn't tell you I came from such a wealthy family. It was important for me to make it on my own. I didn't want my father's name opening any doors for me.'

'You've certainly made a name for yourself in your own right,' Natalie said. 'You have twice the wealth of your father, or so I've heard.'

'For someone who says they have no interest in what I do or who I see, you certainly know a lot about me,' he said with a sardonic smile.

She ignored his comment and picked up her glass again, took a sip. 'What have you told your family about me?' she asked.

'A version of the truth,' he said.

Natalie's eyes came back to his. 'The truth about you hating me and wanting revenge?' she asked with an arch look.

His dark brown eyes gleamed. 'I could hardly tell my parents I hate you, now, could I?'

'What *did* you tell them?'

His eyes kept on holding hers. 'I told them I had never stopped loving you,' he said.

She moistened her lips. 'And they...believed you?'

'They seemed to,' he said. 'Although the real test will be when they see us together. My mother, in particular, is a hard person to fool. You'll have to be on your toes with her.'

Natalie felt her insides quake at the thought of interacting with his parents and other members of his family. How would she do it? How would she play the role of a happy bride without revealing the truth of how things were between them? How long before someone guessed? How long before it was splashed all over the newspapers?

'Why do we have to get married?' she asked. 'Why couldn't we just have an...an affair?'

Those unfathomable brown eyes measured hers. 'Is that what you want?' he asked. 'An affair?'

She ran her tongue over her lips again. 'No more than I want to marry you. I was just making a point,' she said. 'It seems a bit over the top to go to all the trouble of getting married when ultimately we know it's going to end in divorce.'

'You seem very sure it will end in divorce,' he said.

Natalie's heart fluttered like fast moving wings against her breastbone. 'You can't want to be tied to me indefinitely?'

His eyes moved over her leisurely. 'Who knows? You might like being married to me,' he said. 'There will be numerous benefits to wearing my ring and bearing my name.'

She sat up like a puppet suddenly jerked backwards. 'I don't want your name,' she said. 'I'm perfectly happy with my own.'

A steely glint came into his eyes. 'You will take my name,' he said. 'And you will be proud of it.'

She glowered at him, her whole body trembling with anger. 'I will *not* change my name.'

Angelo's eyes warred with hers. 'You will do what I tell you to do,' he said, his voice low but no less forceful.

Natalie stood up so abruptly her chair knocked against the one behind it. Every eye turned to look at her but she was beyond caring. She tossed her napkin down on the table and scooped her purse up with the other.

'Find yourself another wife,' she said, and stormed out.

A camera went off in her face as soon as she stepped outside the restaurant.

'Miss Armitage?' A journalist pushed a microphone close. 'Can we have an exclusive on your current relationship with Angelo Bellandini?'

Natalie tried to avoid the reporter, but another member of the paparazzi cut her off as she tried to escape.

'We notice you're not wearing an engagement ring,' he said. 'Does that mean the wedding's off?'

'I…'

Angelo's arm came around her protectively and he gently led her away from the throng. 'Please give my fiancée some space,' he said.

'Mr Bellandini, do you have a comment to make on your engagement to Miss Armitage?' the first journalist asked.

Angelo's arm tightened around her waist a fraction. 'The wedding is going ahead as planned,' he said. 'I have an engagement ring already picked out for Natalie. I am giving it to her tonight when we get home. Now, please leave us to celebrate our engagement in privacy.'

Natalie was ushered to Angelo's car without further intrusion from the press. She sat back in her seat, her fingers white-knuckled around her purse.

'Don't *ever* do that again,' Angelo said as he fired the engine.

She threw him a cutting glance. 'I am not going to be ordered around by you.'

His hands gripped the steering wheel as tightly as she was clutching her purse. His knuckles looked as if they were going to burst through the skin.

'I will not tolerate you flouncing out on me like a spoilt child,' he said through gritted teeth. 'Do you have no sense of propriety? You do realise that little scene will be all over the papers tomorrow? What were you thinking?'

Natalie gave her head a toss. 'I'm not going to be bullied into changing my name.'

'Fine,' he said. 'It's obviously a sore point with you.

I'm prepared to compromise. I should've realised how important it was to you. It's your trademark.' He paused for a beat. 'I'm sorry.'

She slowly loosened her grip on her purse. 'Are the press always that intrusive?' she asked.

He let out a breath in a sigh. 'I hardly notice it any more,' he said. 'But, yes, they are. It won't last for ever. They'll lose interest once we're married.'

Natalie frowned as she looked at him. 'I hope people don't think I'm marrying you for your money.'

His lips lifted in the slightest of smiles. 'No, *cara*, they'll think it's my body you are after.'

She turned away to stare at the passing scenery, her lower body flickering with a pulse she had thought long ago quelled. 'I'm not going to sleep with you, Angelo,' she said.

'Are you saying that to convince me or yourself?' he asked.

Natalie couldn't have answered either way, so she changed the subject. 'Have you really got an engagement ring?' she asked.

'I have.'

'Do you not think I might have liked to choose it for myself?'

He threw her an exasperated look. 'In my family it's traditional for the man to choose the engagement ring,' he said.

She toyed with the catch on her purse for a moment or two. 'It's not the same one you bought five years ago, is it?' she asked.

'No,' he said.

She sneaked a glance at him but his expression was inscrutable. 'Did you give it to someone else?' she asked. 'As a present or something?'

He brought the car to a standstill outside her house before he answered. 'I donated it to a charity for their silent auction,' he said. 'There's some lucky girl out there now wearing a ring that cost more than most people's houses.'

Natalie chewed at the inside of her mouth. 'I never asked you to spend that amount of money on me.'

His swung his gaze to hers. 'No, you didn't, did you?' he said. 'But then it wasn't money you wanted from me, was it?'

She couldn't hold his look. 'I've seen what money can do to people,' she said. 'It changes them, and not always for the good.'

She felt his gaze studying her for endless seconds. 'What have you told your parents about us?' he asked.

She pressed her lips together. 'Not much.'

'How much?'

She looked at him again. 'It was my mother's idea for me to come and see you,' she said. 'I only did it for her sake.'

'And Lachlan's, presumably?'

Her eyes fell away from his. 'Yes…'

The silence stretched interminably.

'Are you going to ask me in?' he asked.

She gave him a pert look. 'Are you going to come in even if I don't?'

He brushed an idle finger down the curve of her cheek, his eyes focussed on her mouth, his lips curved upwards in a half-smile. 'If you don't want me then all you have to do is say so.'

I do want you.

The words were like drumbeats inside her head.

I want you. I want you. I want you.

She locked out that traitorous voice and pasted an

indifferent look on her face. 'Are you staying in town overnight?' she asked.

'No,' he said. 'I was hoping you'd offer me a bed for the night.'

Natalie felt her heart give a hard, sharp kick. 'I don't think that's such a good idea.'

'Why not?'

'Because… Because…'

'The press will think it odd if I don't stay with you,' he said, before she could think of an excuse. 'I'm not sure if you've noticed, but a car followed us back here. It's parked behind the red car.'

She checked in the side mirror. There was a man sitting behind the wheel with a camera's telephoto lens trained in their direction. Panic gripped her by the throat. Was this how it was going to be? Would she be hounded like a terrified fox with nowhere to hide?

Angelo opened his door and came around to where she was sitting, frozen in dread.

'He'll move on once we're inside,' he said. 'Just try to act naturally.'

Natalie got out of the car and allowed him to take her hand. She felt the strong grip of his fingers as they curled around hers. It was the same feeling she'd had when he had put his arm around her waist earlier.

She felt protected.

'Give me your keys,' he said.

She handed them over. 'It's the big brass one,' she said.

He unlocked the door and held it open for her to pass through. 'How long have you lived here?' he asked as he closed the door.

'Three and a half years.'

'Why Scotland? I thought you said you grew up in Gloucestershire?'

'My mother is a Scot,' she said. 'She grew up in the seaside village of Crail in Fife. I spent a lot of holidays there with my grandparents when I was young.'

'You didn't tell me that before.'

She gave a shrug as she placed her purse on the hall table. 'It didn't seem important.'

'What else didn't you tell me that didn't seem important?'

Natalie turned away from his probing look. 'Do you want a drink or something?'

He stalled her by placing a hand on her arm. 'Tatty?'

She looked down at his hand. How dark and masculine it looked against her paler skin. It dredged up memories she didn't want to resurface. She felt the rumble of them like tectonic plates rubbing against each other. An earthquake of sensation threatened to spill out like lava. She felt the heat of it bubbling like a furnace inside her.

'I asked you not to call me that,' she said.

His hand moved along her arm in a gentle caress. 'I don't always do what I'm told,' he said. 'I like bending the rules to suit me.'

Natalie tried to pull away but his fingers subtly tightened. She met his gaze—so dark and mesmerising—so in control. He knew he had her where he wanted her. She was at his mercy. Lachlan's freedom and future depended on her. Angelo knew she would not do anything to jeopardise it. Her little temper tantrum back at the restaurant had achieved nothing. He would always come after her and remind her of what was at stake.

'Why are you doing this?' she asked. 'You must know how it's going to end.'

His hooded gaze drifted to her mouth. 'I don't care how it ends,' he said. 'This is about the here and now.'

She looked at his mouth. Oh, how she wanted to feel those firm lips move against hers! She remembered the heat; she remembered the blistering passion that burned like a taper all over her flesh. She remembered the sexy thrust of his tongue as it came in search of hers.

Her breath caught in her throat as she felt the breeze of his breath skate over her lips. He lowered his mouth to just above hers. She swept her tongue over her lips, wanting him, aching for him to make the first move.

'Go on,' he said, in a low, husky, spine-melting tone. 'I know you want to.'

Natalie's stomach shifted like a speeding skater suddenly facing a sheet of broken ice. Could he read her so well even after all this time? She fought for composure, for self-control, for anything.

'You're mistaken,' she said coolly. 'I don't want any such thing.'

He brushed a finger over her tingling bottom lip. 'Liar.'

It took all of her resolve and then some to step back, but somehow she did it. She moved to the other side of the room, barricading herself behind one of the sofas set in the middle of the room. 'I think you should leave,' she said.

'Why?' he asked. 'Because you don't trust yourself around me?'

She sent him an arctic look. 'I'm not going to be a slave to your desires.'

'Is that what you think you'll be?' he asked. 'What about your own desires? You have them. You can deny them all you like but they're still there. I can feel it when I touch you.'

'What we had five years ago is gone,' Natalie said. 'You can't make it come back just to suit you.'

'It never went away,' he said. 'You wanted it to, but it didn't. You were scared of the next step, weren't you? You were scared of the commitment of marriage. You're still scared. What I'd like to know is why.'

'Get out.'

'I'm not going until I give you this.' He took a jeweller's box from inside his jacket pocket. But rather than come over to her he simply set it down on the coffee table. It reminded her of a gauntlet being laid down between two opponents.

'I'll have a car sent to collect you on Tuesday,' he said. 'Pack enough clothes for a week. We'll be expected to go on a honeymoon. If you e-mail me a list of the people you wish to invite to the ceremony I'll have my secretary deal with it.'

'What do you want me to wear?' she asked. 'Sackcloth and ashes?'

'You can wear what you like,' he said. 'It makes no difference to me. But do keep in mind that there will be photographers everywhere.'

'Do you really expect me to pack up my life here and follow you about the globe like some lovesick little fool?' she asked.

'We will divide our time between your place and mine,' he said. 'I'm based in London, but I plan to spend a bit of time in Sorrento until the development is near completion. I'm prepared to be flexible. I understand you have a business to run.'

She gave him a petulant look. 'What if I don't want you to share my house?'

'Get used to it, Natalie. I will share your house and a whole lot more before the ink is dry on our marriage certificate.' He went to the door. 'I'll see you on Tuesday.'

Natalie didn't touch the jeweller's box until he had left. She stood looking at it for a long time before she picked it up and opened it. Inside was an art deco design triple diamond ring. It was stunningly beautiful. She took it out of its velvet home and slipped it on her finger. She couldn't have chosen better herself. It was neither too loose nor too tight—a perfect ring for an imperfect relationship.

She wondered how long it would be before she would be giving it back.

CHAPTER FOUR

NATALIE was in a state of high anxiety by the time Tuesday came around.

She hadn't eaten for three days. She had barely slept. She had been dry retching at the thought of getting on a plane to Italy.

Angelo had called her each day, but she hadn't revealed anything of what she was going through. He had assured her Lachlan was out of harm's way. Her parents had called too, and expressed their satisfaction with the way things had turned out. Her father was greatly relieved that the family name hadn't been sullied by Lachlan's antics. Angelo had miraculously made the nasty little episode disappear, for which Adrian Armitage was immensely grateful. He'd made no mention of Natalie's role in fixing things. She had expected no less from him, given he had never shown an interest in her welfare, but she was particularly annoyed with her mother, who hadn't even asked her how she felt about marrying Angelo. But then Isla had married Natalie's father for money and prestige. Love hadn't come into it at all.

She felt annoyed too at having to lie to her friends—in particular Isabel. But strangely enough Isabel had accepted the news of her marriage with barely a blink of an eye. Her friend had said how she had always thought Natalie had unresolved feelings for Angelo since she hadn't dated all that seriously since. She thought Natalie's aversion to marriage and commitment had stemmed from her break up with Angelo. Natalie hadn't had the heart to put Isabel straight. As close as she was to her, she had never told Isabel about the circumstances surrounding Liam's death.

Natalie heard a car pull up outside her house. Her stomach did another somersault and a clammy sweat broke out over her brow. She walked to the door on legs that felt like wet cotton wool. It wasn't a uniformed driver standing there but Angelo himself.

'I…I just have to get my bag…' she said, brushing a loose strand of sticky hair back behind her ear.

Angelo narrowed his gaze. 'Are you all right?'

'I'm fine,' she said, averting her eyes.

He put a hand on her shoulder and turned her to look at him. 'You're deathly pale,' he said. 'Are you ill?'

Natalie swallowed the gnarly knot of panic in her throat. 'I have some pills to take.' She rummaged in her bag for the anxiety medication her doctor had prescribed. 'I won't be a minute.'

She went to the kitchen for a glass of water and Angelo followed her. He took the packet of pills from her and read the label. 'Do you really need to take these?' he asked.

'Give them to me,' she said, reaching for them. 'I should've taken them an hour ago.'

He frowned as he handed them to her. 'Do you take them regularly?'

She shook her head as she swallowed a couple of pills. 'No,' she said. 'Only in an emergency.'

He was still frowning as he led her out to the car. 'When did you develop your fear of flying?' he asked.

'Ages ago,' she said.

'What caused it?' he asked. 'Rough turbulence or a mid-air incident?'

She shrugged. 'Can't remember.'

His dark gaze searched hers. 'When was the last time you flew?'

'Can we get going?' she asked. 'I don't want to fall asleep in the car. You'll have to carry me on board.'

Angelo glanced at Natalie every now and again as he drove to the airport. She was not quite so pale now the medication had settled her nerves, but she still looked fragile. Her cheeks looked hollow, as if she had recently lost weight, and her eyes were shadowed.

Her concern over her brother was well founded. He had struck a deal with Lachlan, but already Lachlan was pushing against the boundaries Angelo had set in place. The staff at a very expensive private rehab clinic had called him three times in the last week to inform him about Lachlan's erratic and at times uncontrollable behaviour. He had organised a therapist to have extra sessions with him, but so far there had been no miraculous breakthrough. It seemed Lachlan Armitage was a very angry young man, hell-bent on self-destruction.

Speaking with Natalie's father had made Angelo realise how frustrating it must be to have a child who, no matter how much you loved and provided for him, refused to co-operate. Adrian Armitage had hinted at similar trouble with Natalie. Apparently her stubborn streak had caused many a scene in the Armitage household over the years. In spite of all of her father's efforts to get close to her she had wilfully defied him whenever she could. Angelo wondered if it was a cultural thing. He had been brought up strictly, but fairly. His parents had commanded respect, but they had more than earned it with their dedication and love for him. He hoped to do the same for his own children one day.

He turned off the engine once he had parked and gently touched Natalie on the shoulder. 'Hey, sleepy-head,' he said. 'Time to get going.'

She blinked and sat up straighter. 'Oh... Right...'

He put an arm around her waist as he led her on board his private jet a short time later. She was agitated and edgy, but he managed to get her to take a seat and put the belt on.

'Can I have a drink?' she asked.

'Sure,' he said. 'What would you like?'

'White wine,' she said.

'Are you sure it's a good idea to combine alcohol with those pills?' he asked.

She gave him a surly look. 'I'm not a child.'

'No, but you're under my protection,' he said. 'I don't want you getting ill, or losing consciousness or something.'

She started chewing her nails as the pilot pulled back. Angelo took her hand away from her mouth and covered it with his. 'You'll be fine, *cara*,' he said. 'You were in far more danger driving to the airport than you ever will be in the air.'

She shifted restively, her eyes darting about like a spooked thoroughbred's. 'I want to get off,' she said. 'Please—can you tell the pilot to stop? I want to get off.'

Angelo put his arm around her and brought her close against him. 'Shh, *mia piccola*,' he soothed. 'Concentrate on your breathing. In and out. In and out. That's right. Nice and slow.'

She squeezed her eyes shut and lowered her head to his chest. He stroked the silk of her hair, talking to her in the same calm voice. It took a lot longer than he expected but finally she relaxed against him. She slept for most of the journey and only woke up just as they were coming to land in Rome.

'There,' he said. 'You did it. That wasn't so bad, was it?'

She nodded vaguely and brushed the hair back off her face. 'Have I got time to use the bathroom?'

'Sure,' he said. 'Do you want me to come with you?'

Her cheeks pooled with colour. 'No, thank you.'

He gave her a mocking smile. 'Maybe next time, *si*?'

The press had obviously been given a tip-off somewhere between their arrival at the airport and Angelo's family villa in Rome. Natalie watched in dismay as photographers surged towards Angelo's chauffeur-driven car.

'Don't worry,' he said as he helped her out of the car. 'I'll handle their questions.'

Within a few moments Angelo had managed to satisfy the press's interest and sent them on their way.

An older man opened the front door of the villa and greeted Angelo. 'Your parents are in the salon, Signor Bellandini.'

'*Grazie*, Pasquale,' he said. 'Natalie, this is Pasquale. He has been working for my family for many years.'

'I'm very pleased to meet you,' Natalie said.

'Welcome,' Pasquale said. 'It is very nice to see Signor Bellandini happy at last.'

'Come,' Angelo said, guiding her with a hand resting in the curve of her back. 'My parents will be keen to meet you.'

If they were so keen, why hadn't they been at the

door to greet her instead of the elderly servant? Natalie thought bitterly to herself. But clearly there was a different protocol in the upper classes of Italian society. And Sandro and Francesca Bellandini were nothing if not from the very top shelf of the upper class.

Natalie could see where Angelo got his height and looks from as soon as she set eyes on his father. While an inch or two shorter than his son, Sandro had the same dark brown eyes and lean, rangy build. His hair was still thick and curly but it was liberally streaked with grey, giving him a distinguished air that was as compelling as it was intimidating.

Francesca, on the other hand, was petite, and her demeanour outwardly demure, but her keen hazel eyes missed nothing. Natalie felt them move over her in one quick assessing glance, noting her hair and make-up, the style and make of her clothes, the texture of her skin and the state of her figure.

'This is Natalie, my fiancée,' Angelo said. 'Natalie— my parents, Sandro and Francesca.'

'Welcome to the family.' Francesca was the first to speak. 'Angelo has told us so much about you. I am sorry we didn't meet you five years ago. We would've told him he was a fool for letting you go—*si*, Sandro?'

'*Si,*' Sandro said, taking her hand once his wife had relinquished it. 'You are very welcome indeed.'

Angelo's arm came back around her waist. 'I'll see that Natalie is settled in upstairs before we join you for a celebratory drink.'

'Maria has made up the Venetian room for you both,' Francesca said. 'I didn't see the point in separating you. You've been apart too long, no?'

Natalie glanced at Angelo, but he was smiling at his

mother. 'That was very thoughtful of you, *Mamma,*' he said.

Natalie had to wait until they were upstairs and alone before she could vent her spleen. 'I bet you did that deliberately,' she said.

'Did what?'

'Don't play the guileless innocent with me,' she flashed back. 'You knew your mother would put us in the same room, didn't you?'

'On the contrary. I thought she would go old-fashioned on me and put us at opposite ends of the villa,' he said. 'I told you she's incredibly insightful. She must have sensed how hot you are for me.'

Natalie glared at him. 'I'm not sharing that bed with you.'

'Fine,' he said unbuttoning his shirt. 'I'll let you have the floor.'

She frowned at him. 'What are you doing?'

He pulled his shirt out of the waistband of his trousers. 'I'm getting changed.'

Her eyes went the flat plane of his abdomen. He looked amazing—so masculine, so taut, so magnificently fit and tanned and virile. She swung away and went to look out of the windows overlooking the gardens.

'Why did you let your parents think it was you who ended our affair five years ago?' she asked.

'I didn't want you to get off to a bad start with them,' he said. 'I'm their only child. Parents can be funny about things like that.'

Natalie turned around. He was only wearing black underwear now. The fabric clung to him lovingly. Her insides clenched with greedy fistfuls of desire. She had kissed and tasted every inch of his body. She had taken him in her mouth, ruthlessly tasting him until he had collapsed with release. She had felt him move deep within her. She had felt his essence spill inside her. She had been as brazen as she could be with him and yet still he had always been a step ahead of her. He had pushed her to the limit time and time again. Her flesh shivered in memory of his touch. Her spine tingled and her belly fluttered. She drew in a breath as she saw his gaze run over her. Was he too thinking of the red-hot passion they had shared?

'I don't expect you to take the blame,' she said. 'I'm not ashamed of breaking off our relationship. I was too young to get married.'

'That won't cut it with my mother, I'm afraid,' he said. 'She was barely sixteen when she fell in love with my father. She has never looked at another man since.'

'Is your father faithful to her?'

He frowned. 'What makes you ask that?'

Natalie lifted a shoulder up and down. 'They've been together a long time. It's not uncommon for a man to stray.'

'My father takes his marriage vows seriously,' he said. 'He is exactly like my grandfather in that.'

'And what about you, Angelo?' she asked. 'Will you follow in their honourable footsteps, or will you have your little bits on the side if I don't come up trumps?'

He came over to where she was standing. Stopped just in front of her. So close she could feel her body swaying towards him like a compass searching for magnetic north. She fought against the desire to close the minuscule distance. She stood arrow-straight, stiff to the point of discomfort. Her heart was racing; the hammer blows were making her giddy, her breathing shallow and uneven.

Her resolve, God help her, was crumbling.

Angelo slipped a warm hand behind her head at the nape of her neck setting off a shower of sensation beneath the surface of her sensitive skin.

'Why do you fight with yourself so much?' he asked.

Natalie pressed her lips together. 'I'm fighting you, not myself.'

His fingers moved through her hair in a spine-tingling caress. 'We both want the same thing, *cara*,' he said. 'Connection, intimacy, satisfaction.'

She could feel her resolve slipping even further out of her control. Why did he have to look so damned gorgeous? Why did he have to have such melting brown eyes? Why did he have to have such amazing hands that made her flesh tingle with sensation? Why did he have to have such a tempting mouth?

For God's sake, why didn't he throw her backwards caveman-style on the bed and ravish her?

In the end it was impossible to tell who had closed the distance between their bodies. Suddenly she felt the hard ridge of his erection pressing against her belly. It was like putting a match to a decade of dried-out tinder. She felt the flames erupt beneath her flesh. They licked along every nerve pathway, from the top of her scalp to her toes.

Her mouth met his in a combative duel that had no hint of romance or tenderness about it. It was all about lust—primal, ravenous lust—that was suddenly let loose after being restrained for far too long. She felt the scorch of his lips as they ground against hers. And then his tongue thrust boldly through the seam of her lips, making her insides flip over in delight. Her tongue tangled with his, fighting for supremacy, but he wouldn't give in. She felt the scrape of her teeth against his; she even tasted blood but couldn't be sure whose it was. She fed off his mouth greedily, rapaciously, and little whimpers of pleasure sounded deep in her throat as he varied the speed and pressure.

He crushed her to him, one of his hands ruthlessly tugging her top undone so he could access her breast. She felt her achingly tight nipple rubbing against his palm. A wave of longing besieged her. She felt it flickering like a pulse between her thighs. She felt the honeyed moistness of her body preparing for his possession. She rubbed up against him intimately, the feminine heart of her on fire, aching, pulsing, contracting with a need so great it was overwhelming.

He kept kissing her relentlessly, his tongue diving for hers, conquering it with each and every sensual stroke. Her lips felt swollen but she didn't care. She kissed him back with just as much passion, nipping at him with her teeth in between stroking him with her tongue. He tasted just as she remembered him: minty and fresh and devastatingly, irresistibly male.

He tore his mouth from hers to suckle on her breast, his tongue swirling around her areola and over her nipple until her back arched in pleasure. She knew it would take very little to send her up into the stratosphere. She could feel the tremors at her core, the tension building and building, until she was close to begging him to satisfy that delicious, torturous ache.

He brought his mouth back to hers—a slower kiss this time. He took his time exploring her mouth, his tongue teasing hers rather than subduing it. She melted like honey in a hothouse. Her arms went around his neck. Her hands delved into the thick denseness of his hair. Her throbbing pelvis was flush against the hardness of his.

He raised his mouth from hers, his breathing heavy, his eyes dark and heavy-lidded and smouldering with desire. 'Tell me you want me,' he commanded.

Natalie was jolted out of his sensual spell with a resurgence of her pride. 'I don't want you,' she lied.

He gave a deep and very masculine-sounding mocking laugh. 'I could prove that for the lie that it is just by slipping my hand between your legs.'

She tried to back away but he held her fast. 'Get your hands off me,' she said through gritted teeth.

He slowly slid his hands down the length of her arms, his fingers encircling her wrists like handcuffs. 'You will come to me, *cara*, just like you did in the past,' he said. 'I know you too well.'

She held his gaze defiantly. 'You don't know me at all,' she said. 'You might know your way around my body, but you know nothing of my heart.'

'That's because you won't let anyone in, will you?' he said. 'You push everyone away when they get too close. Your father told me how difficult you are.'

Natalie's mouth dropped open in outrage. 'You discussed *me* with my father?'

His hands fell away from her wrists, his expression masked. 'We had a couple of conversations, yes,' he said.

'About what?'

'I asked for your hand in marriage.'

She gave a derisive laugh. 'That was rather draconian of you, wasn't it? And also hypocritical—because you wouldn't have let the little matter of my father's permission stand in the way of what you wanted, now, would you?'

'I thought it was the right thing to do,' he said. 'I

would've liked to meet him face to face but he was abroad on business.'

Natalie could just imagine the 'business' her father was working on. His latest project was five-foot-ten with bottle-blonde hair and breasts you could serve a dinner party off.

'I'm sure he didn't hesitate in handing me over to your care,' she said. 'I'm surprised he didn't offer to pay you for the privilege.'

His gaze remained steady on hers, dark and penetrating but giving nothing away. 'We also discussed Lachlan's situation.'

'I take it he didn't offer to postpone his *business* in order to be by Lachlan's side and sort things out?'

'I told him to stay away,' he said. 'Sometimes parents can get in the way when it comes to situations like this. Your father has done all he can for your brother. It's time to step back and let others take charge.'

'Which you just couldn't wait to do, because it gave you the perfect foothold to force me back into your life,' she said, shooting him a resentful glare.

Those piercing brown eyes refused to let hers go. 'You came to me, Natalie, not the other way around.'

A thought slipped into her mind like the thin curl of smoke beneath a door. 'My father was the one who contacted you, wasn't he?' she said, her eyes narrowed in suspicion. 'I only came to you because my mother begged me to. I would never have come to you otherwise. *He* put her up to it.'

'Your father expressed his concern for you when we spoke,' he said. 'It seems it's not only your brother with an attitude problem.'

Natalie stalked to the other side of the bedroom, her arms around her body so tightly she felt her ribs creak in protest. Her anger was boiling like a cauldron inside her. She wanted to explode. She wanted to hit out at him, at the world, at the cruel injustice of life. The thought of Angelo discussing her with her father was repugnant to her. She hated thinking of how that conversation would have played out.

Her father would have painted her as a wilful and defiant child with no self-discipline. He would have laid it on thickly, relaying anecdote after anecdote about how she had disobeyed him and made life difficult for him almost from the day she had been born. He would not have told of how he had wanted a son first, and how she had ruined his plans by being born a girl. He would not have told of his part in provoking her, goading her into black moods and tempers until he finally broke her spirit. He would not have told of how his philosophy of parenting was 'might is right', how tyranny took precedence over tolerance, ridicule and shame over support and guidance. He would not have told of how he had used harsh physical discipline when gentle corrective words would have achieved a much better outcome.

No, he would have portrayed himself as a long-suffering devoted father who was at his wits' end over his wayward offspring.

He would not have mentioned Liam.

Liam's death was a topic *no one* mentioned. It was as if he had never existed. None of his toys or clothes were at the family mansion. Her father had forced her mother to remove them as soon as Lachlan had been born. The photos of Liam's infancy and toddlerhood were in an album in a cupboard that was securely locked and never opened. Natalie's only photo of her baby brother was the one she had found in the days after his funeral, when everyone had been distraught and distracted. She had kept it hidden until she had bought her house in Edinburgh.

But for all her father's efforts to erase the tragedy of Liam's short life his ghost still haunted them all. Every time Natalie visited her parents—which was rare these days—she felt his presence. She saw his face in Lachlan's. She heard him in her sleep. Every year she had night terrors as the anniversary of his death came close.

With an enormous effort she garnered her self-control, and once she was sure she had her emotions securely locked and bolted down she slowly turned and faced Angelo. 'I'm sure you found that conversation very enlightening,' she said.

His expression was hard to read. 'Your father cares for you very deeply,' he said. 'Like all parents, he and your mother only want the best for you.'

Natalie kept her mouth straight, even though she longed to curl her lip. 'My father obviously thinks you're the best for me,' she said. 'And as for my mother—well, she wouldn't dream of contradicting him. So it's happy families all round, isn't it?'

He studied her for a heartbeat, his eyes holding hers in a searching, probing manner. 'I'm going to have a shower,' he said. 'My parents will have gone to a great deal of trouble over dinner. Please honour them by dressing and behaving appropriately.'

'Contrary to what my father probably told you, I *do* actually know how to behave in company,' she said to his back as he went towards the *en suite* bathroom.

He turned around and meshed his gaze with hers. 'I'm on your side, *cara*,' he said, with unexpected gentleness.

Her eyes stung with the sudden onset of tears. She

blinked and got them back where they belonged: con-
cealed, blocked, and stoically, strenuously denied. She
gave a toss of her head and walked back to the window overlooking the gardens. But she didn't let out her
breath until she heard the click of the bathroom door
indicating Angelo had gone.

Angelo was putting on some cufflinks when he heard
Natalie come out of the dressing room. He turned and
looked at her, his breath catching in his chest at the sight
of her dressed in a classic knee length black dress and
patent leather four-inch heels. Her hair was pulled back
in an elegant knot at the back of her head, giving her a
regal air. She was wearing diamond and pearl droplet
earrings and a matching necklace. Her make-up was
subtle, but it highlighted the dark blue of her eyes and
the creamy texture of her skin and model-like cheekbones. Her perfume drifted towards him—a bewitch-
ing blend of the wintry bloom of lily of the valley and
the hot summer fragrance of honeysuckle. A perfect
summation of her complex character: ice-maiden and
sultry siren.

How could someone so beautiful on the outside be
capable of the things her father had said about her? It
was worrying him—niggling at him like a toothache.
The more time he spent with her, the more he found new
aspects to her character that intrigued him.

Yes, she was wilful and defiant. Yes, she had a streak
of independence. Yes, she could be incredibly stubborn.

But she clearly loved her brother and was prepared
to go to extraordinary lengths to help him. How did
that fit in with Adrian Armitage's assessment of her as
totally selfish and self-serving?

'You look like you just stepped off a New York City catwalk,' he said.

She lifted a slim shoulder dismissively. 'This dress is three seasons old,' she said. 'I bought it on sale for a fraction of the cost.'

'I like your hair like that.'

'It needs cutting,' she said, touching a hand to one of her earrings. 'This is a good way to hide the split ends.'

'Why don't you like compliments?' he asked. 'You always deflect them. You used to do that five years ago. I thought it was because you were young back then, but you're still doing it.'

She stopped fiddling with her earring to look at him, her chin coming up. 'Compliment me all you like,' she said. 'I can handle it.'

'You're beautiful.'

'Thank you.'

'And extremely intelligent.'

She gave a little mock bow. 'Thank you.'

'And you have the most amazing body,' he said.

High on her cheekbones twin pools of delicate rose appeared, and her eyes moved out of reach of his. 'I haven't been to the gym in months.'

'You're meant to say thank you—not make excuses,' he pointed out.

She brought her gaze back. 'Thank you.'

'You're the most intriguing person I know.'

A mask fell over her face like a curtain dropping over a stage. 'You need to get out a little more, Angelo,' she said.

'You have secrets in your eyes.'

She stilled as if every cell in her body had been snap frozen. But then, just as quickly she relaxed her pose.

'We all have our secrets,' she said lightly. 'I wonder what some of yours are?'

'Who gave you that jewellery?' he asked.

She put a hand to her throat, where her necklace rested. 'I bought it for myself,' she said.

'Do you still have the locket I gave you from that street fair we went to?'

She dropped her hand from her neck and reached for her purse. 'Your parents will be wondering what's keeping us,' she said.

'My parents will think we've been catching up on lost time.'

Her cheeks fired again. 'I hope they don't expect me to speak Italian, because I'm hopeless at it.'

'They won't expect you to do anything you're not comfortable with,' he said. 'They're keen to welcome you as the daughter they never had.'

'I hope I live up to their lofty expectations,' she said, frowning a little. 'But then, I guess no one is ever going to be good enough for the parents of an only child.'

'I'm sure they will grow to love you if you show them who you really are,' he said.

'Yeah, like *that's* going to work,' she said, and picked up her wrap and wound it round her shoulders.

Angelo frowned. 'Why do you say that?'

'No one really gets to be who they truly are on the inside, do they?' she said. 'We all fall into line because of cultural conditioning and family expectation. None of us can say what we really want to say or do what we really want to do. We're hemmed in by parameters imposed on us by other people and the society we live in.'

'What would you do or say if those parameters weren't there?' he asked.

She gave one of her dismissive shrugs. 'What would be the point?' she asked. 'No one listens anyway.'

'I'm listening,' he said.

Her eyes fell away from his. 'We shouldn't keep your parents waiting.'

He brought her chin up with his finger and thumb. 'Don't shut me out, *cara*,' he said. 'For God's sake, talk to me. I'm tired of this don't-come-too-close-to-me game you keep playing.'

Her expression flickered with a host of emotions. He saw them pass through her eyes like a burgeoning tide. They rippled over her forehead and tightened her jaw, but she spoke none of them out loud.

'You won't let me in, will you?' he said.

'There's nothing *in* there.'

'I don't believe that,' he said. 'I know you try and pretend otherwise, but you have a soft heart and you won't let anyone get near it. Why? Why are you so determined to deny yourself human connection and intimacy?'

She stepped out of his hold and gave him a hardened look. 'Didn't my father tell you?' she said. 'I'm a lost cause. I'm beyond redemption. I have a streak of selfishness and self-preservation that overrides everything else. I care for no one but myself.'

'If that is so then why have you agreed to sacrifice yourself for your brother's sake?' he asked.

There was a hint of movement at her slim throat, as if she had tried to disguise a swallow. 'Lachlan isn't like me,' she said. 'He's sensitive and vulnerable. He doesn't know how to take care of himself yet, but he will. He just needs more time.'

'You're paying a very high price for his learning curve.'

She met his gaze levelly. 'I've paid higher.'

Angelo tried to break her gaze down with the laser force of his but she was indomitable. It was like trying to melt a wall of steel with a child's birthday cake candle. 'I won't give up on you, Natalie,' he said. 'I don't care how long it takes. I will not give up until I see what's written on your heart.'

'Good luck with that,' she said airily, and sashayed to the door. She stopped and addressed him over her shoulder. 'Are you coming or not?'

CHAPTER FIVE

NATALIE was handed a glass of champagne as soon as she entered the salon on Angelo's arm.

'This is such a happy occasion for us,' Francesca said. 'We were starting to wonder if Angelo would ever settle down, weren't we, Sandro?'

Angelo's father gave a benign smile as he raised his glass. 'Indeed,' he said. 'But we always knew he would only ever marry for love. It is a Bellandini tradition, after all.'

'Isn't it also twenty-first century tradition to do so?' Natalie asked.

'Well, yes, of course,' Francesca said. 'But that's not to say that certain families don't occasionally orchestrate meetings between their young ones to hurry things along. Parents often have a feel for these things.'

'I'm not sure parents should get involved in their children's lives to that extent,' Natalie said. 'Surely once someone is an adult they should be left to decide what and who is right for them?'

Sandro's dark brown eyes glinted as he addressed his son. 'I can see you have chosen a wife with spirit, Angelo,' he said. 'Life is so much more exciting with a woman who has a mind of her own.'

Francesca gave Sandro a playful tap on the arm.

'You've done nothing but complain for the last thirty-six years about *my* spirit.'

Sandro took her hand and kissed it gallantly. 'I adore your spirit, *tesoro mio*,' he said. 'I worship it.'

Natalie couldn't help comparing her parents' relationship to Angelo's parents'. Her parents spoke to each other on a need basis. She couldn't remember the last time they had touched. They certainly didn't look at each other with love shining from their eyes. They could barely be in the same room together.

'Papa, Mamma,' Angelo said. 'You're embarrassing Natalie.'

Francesca came over and looped an arm through one of Natalie's. 'Angelo tells me you are a very talented interior designer,' she said. 'I am ashamed that I hadn't seen your soft furnishings range until I searched for it online. I cannot believe what I have been missing. Do you not have an Italian outlet?'

'I've limited my outlets to the UK up until now,' Natalie said.

'But why?' Francesca said. 'Your designs are wonderful.'

'I'm not fond of travelling,' Natalie said. 'I know I should probably do more in terms of networking in Europe...'

'Never mind,' Francesca said, patting her arm reassuringly. 'Angelo will see to it. He is very good at business. You will soon be a household name and I will be immensely proud of you. I will tell everyone you are my lovely daughter-in-law and I will not speak to them ever again unless they buy all of your linen and use all of your treatments in their homes, *si*?'

Natalie thought of her father's dismissal of her latest range as 'too girly' and 'too Parisian'. She felt more affirmed after five minutes with Angelo's mother than she had in a lifetime with her father.

'I'll get my assistant to send you a catalogue,' she said. 'If you want a hand with anything I'd be happy to help.'

'Oh, would you?' Francesca's eyes danced with excitement. 'I've been dying to redecorate the guest rooms. I would *love* your help. It will be a bonding experience, *si*?'

'I'd like that,' Natalie said.

Francesca smiled. 'I have been so nervous about us meeting,' she said. 'But I am happy now. You are perfect for Angelo. You love him very much, no?'

'I... I...'

Francesca squeezed Natalie's forearm. 'I understand,' she said. 'You don't like wearing your heart on your sleeve, *si*? But I can see what you feel for him. I don't need you to say it out loud. You are not the sort of girl who would marry for anything but for love.'

Angelo came over and put an arm around Natalie's waist. 'So you approve, *Mamma*?' he said.

'But of course,' his mother said. 'She is an angel. We will get on famously.'

Dinner was a lively, convivial affair—again very different from meals taken at Natalie's family home. At the Armitage mansion no one spoke unless Adrian Armitage gave permission. It was a pattern from childhood that neither Natalie nor Lachlan had been courageous enough to challenge.

But in the Bellandini household, magnificent and imposing as it was, everyone was encouraged to contribute to the conversation. Natalie didn't say much. She listened and watched as Angelo interacted with his parents. They debated volubly about politics and religion and the state of the economy, but no one got angry or upset, or slammed their fist down on the table. It was like watching a very exciting tennis match. The ball of conversation was hit back and forth, but nothing but good sportsmanship was on show.

After the coffee cups were cleared Angelo placed a gentle hand on the nape of Natalie's neck. 'You will excuse us, *Mamma* and *Papa*?' he said. 'Natalie is exhausted.'

'But of course,' Francesca said.

Sandro got to his feet and joined his wife in kissing Natalie on both cheeks. 'Sleep well, Natalie,' he said. 'It is a very great privilege to welcome you to our family.'

Natalie struggled to keep her overwhelmed emotions back behind the screen she had erected. 'You're very kind...'

Angelo kept his hand at her back all the way upstairs. 'You didn't eat much at dinner,' he said. 'Are you still feeling unwell?'

'No,' she said. 'I'm not a big eater.'

'You're very thin,' he said. 'You seem to have lost even more weight since the day you came to my office.'

She kept her gaze averted as she trudged up the stairs. 'I always lose weight in the summer.'

He held the door of their suite open for her. 'My parents adore you.'

She gave him a vestige of a smile. 'They're lovely people. You're very lucky.'

Angelo closed the door and watched as she removed the clip holding her hair in place. Glossy brunette tresses flowed over her shoulders. He wanted to run his fingers through them, to bury his head in their fragrant mass.

'You can have the bed,' he said. 'I'll sleep in one of the other rooms.'

'Won't your parents think it rather odd if you sleep somewhere else?' she asked, frowning slightly.

'I'll think of some excuse.'

'I'm sure we can manage to share a bed for a night or two,' she said, looking away. 'It's not as if we're out-of-control, hormonally driven teenagers or anything.'

Angelo felt exactly like an out-of-control, hormonally driven teenager, but he thought it best not to say so. He wasn't sure he would be able to sleep a wink with her lying beside him, but he was going to give it a damn good try.

'You use the bathroom first,' he said. 'I have a couple of e-mails to send.'

She gave a vague nod and disappeared into the *ensuite* bathroom.

When he finally came back into the bedroom Natalie was soundly asleep. She barely took up any room in the king-sized bed. He stood looking at her for a long time, wondering where he had gone wrong with her. Had he expected too much too soon? She had only been twenty-one. It was young for the commitment of marriage, but he had been so certain she was the one for him he hadn't stopped to consider she might say no. It had been perhaps a little arrogant of him, but he had never factored in the possibility that she would leave him. All his life he had been given everything he wanted. It was part and parcel of being an only child born to extremely wealthy parents. He had never experienced disappointment or betrayal.

He had her now where he wanted her, but he wasn't happy and neither was she. She was a caged bird. She would not stay confined for long. She would do her duty to save her brother's hide but she would not stay with him indefinitely.

He slipped between the sheets a few minutes later and lay listening to the sound of her soft breathing. He ached to pull her into his arms but he was determined she would come to him of her own volition. He closed his eyes and willed himself to relax.

He was not far off sleep when he felt Natalie stiffen like a board beside him. The bed jolted with the movement of her body as she started to thrash about as if she were possessed by an inner demon. He had never seen her jerk or throw herself about in such a way. He was concerned she was going to hurt herself.

'No!' she cried. 'No! No! No! *Noooo*!'

Angelo reached for her, restraining her flailing arms and legs with the shelter of his body half covering hers. 'Shh, *cara*,' he said softly. 'It's just a bad dream. Shh.'

Her eyes opened wide and she gulped over a sob as she covered her face with her hands. 'Oh, God,' she said. 'I couldn't find him. I couldn't find him.'

He brushed the hair back off her forehead. 'Who couldn't you find, *mia piccola*?' he asked.

She shook her head from side to side, her face still shielded by her hands. 'It was my fault,' she said, the words sounding as if they were scraped out of her throat. 'It was *my* fault.'

He frowned and pulled her hands down from her face. 'What was your fault?'

She blinked and focussed on his face. 'I… I…' She swallowed. 'I—I'm sorry…'

She started to cry, her face crumpling like a sheet of paper snatched up by someone's hand. Big crystal tears popped from her eyes and flowed down her face. He had never seen her cry. He had seen her furiously angry and he had seen her happy, and just about everything in between, but he had never seen her in tears.

'Hey,' he said, blotting each tear as it fell with the pad of his finger. 'It's just a dream, Tatty. It's not real. It's just a horrible nightmare.'

She cried all the harder, great choking sobs that made his own chest feel sore.

'I'm sorry,' she kept saying like a mantra. 'I'm sorry. I'm sorry. I'm sorry.'

'Shh,' he said again. 'There's nothing to be sorry about.' He stroked her face and her hair. 'There…let it go, *cara*. That's my girl. Let it all go.'

Her sobs gradually subsided to hiccups and she finally nestled against his chest and fell into an exhausted sleep. Angelo kept on stroking her hair as the clock worked its way around to dawn.

He could not have slept a wink if he tried.

Natalie opened her eyes and found Angelo's dark, thoughtful gaze trained on her. She had some vague memory of what had passed during the night but it was like looking at something through a cloudy, opaque film.

'I hope I didn't keep you awake,' she said. 'I'm not a very good sleeper.'

'You're certainly very restless,' he said. 'I don't remember you being like that when we were together.'

She focussed her gaze on the white cotton sheet that was pulled up to her chest. 'I sleep much better in the winter.'

'I can see why you choose to live in Scotland.'

She felt a reluctant smile tug at her mouth. 'Maybe I should move to Antarctica or the North Pole.'

'Maybe you should talk to someone about your dreams.'

She got off the bed and snatched up a bathrobe to cover her nightwear. 'Maybe you should mind your own business,' she said, tying the waist strap with unnecessary force.

He got off the bed and came to stand where she was standing. 'Don't push me away, Natalie,' he said. 'Can't you see I'm trying to help you?'

She glared at him, her anger straining like an unbroken horse on a string bridle. 'Back off. I don't need your help. I was perfectly fine until you came along and stuffed everything up. You with your stupid plans for revenge. Who are *you* to sort out my life? You don't know a thing about my life. You just think you can manipulate things to suit you. Go ahead. See if I care.'

She flung herself away, huddling into herself like a porcupine faced with a predator. But her prickly spines felt as if they were pointing the wrong way. She felt every savage poke of them into her sensitive soul.

'Why are you being so antagonistic?' he asked. 'What's happened to make you like this?'

Natalie squeezed her eyes shut as she fought for control. 'I don't need you to psychoanalyse me, Angelo. I don't need you to fix me. I was fine until you barged back into my life.'

'You're not fine,' he said. 'You're far from fine. I want to help you.'

She kept her back turned on him. 'You don't need me to complicate your life. You can have anyone. You don't need me.'

'I do need you,' he said. 'And you need me.'

She felt as if he had reached inside her chest and grasped her heart in his hand and squashed it. She wasn't the right person for him. She could never be the right person for him. Why couldn't he see it? Did she have to spell it out for him?

'You deserve someone who can love you,' she said. 'I'm not capable of that.'

'I don't know what's happened in your life to make you think that, but it's not true,' he said. 'You do care, Natalie. You care about everything, but you keep your feelings locked away where no one can see them.'

She pinched the bridge of her nose until her eyes watered. 'I've stuffed up so many lives.' She sucked in a breath and released it raggedly. 'I've tried to be a good person but sometimes it's just not enough.'

'You *are* a good person,' he said. 'Why are you so damned hard on yourself?'

Natalie felt the anguish of her soul assail her all over again. She had carried this burdensome yoke since she was seven years old. Instead of getting lighter it had become heavier. It had dug down deep into the shoulders of her guilt. She had no hope of shrugging it off. It was like a big, ugly track mark on her soul.

It was with her for life. It was her penance, her punishment.

'When I was a little girl I thought the world was a magical place,' she said. 'I thought if I just wished for something hard enough it would happen.'

'That's the magic of childhood,' he said. 'Every child thinks that.'

'I truly believed if I wanted something badly enough it would come to me,' she said. 'Where did I get that from? Life isn't like that. It's never been like that. It's not like some Hollywood script where everything turns out right in the end. It's pain and sadness and grief at what could have been but wasn't. It's one long journey of relentless suffering.'

'Why do you find life so difficult?' he asked. 'You come from a good family. You have wealth and a roof over your head, food on the table. What is there to be so miserable about? So many people are much worse off.'

She rolled her eyes and headed for the bathroom. 'I don't expect you to understand.'

'Make me understand.'

She turned and looked at him. His dark eyes were so concerned and serious. How could she bear to see him look at her in horror and disgust if she told him the truth? She let out a long sigh and pushed against the door with her hand. 'I'm going to have a shower,' she said. 'I'll see you downstairs.'

Angelo was having coffee in the breakfast room when Natalie came in. She looked cool and composed. There was no sign of the distress he had witnessed during the dark hours of the night and first thing this morning. Her ice maiden persona was back in place.

He rose from the table as she came in and held out a chair for her. 'My mother has organised a shopping morning for you,' he said. 'She'll be with you shortly. She's just seeing to some last-minute things with the housekeeper.'

'But I don't need anything,' she said, frowning as she sat down.

'Aren't you forgetting something?' he asked. 'We're getting married on Saturday.'

Her eyes fell away from his as she placed a napkin over her lap. 'I wasn't planning on going to any trouble over a dress,' she said. 'I have a cream suit that will do.'

'It's not just your wedding, *cara*,' he said. 'It's mine

too. My family and yours are looking forward to celebrating with us. It won't be the same if you turn up in a dress you could wear any old time. I want you to look like a bride.'

A spark of defiance lit her slate-blue gaze as it clashed with his. 'I don't want to look like a meringue,' she said. 'And don't expect me to wear a veil, because I won't.'

Angelo clamped his teeth together to rein in his temper. Was she being deliberately obstructive just to needle him for forcing her hand? He regretted showing his tender side to her last night. She was obviously going to manipulate him to get her own way. Hadn't her father warned him? She was clever at getting what she wanted. She would go to extraordinary lengths to do so.

But then, so would he.

She had met her match in him and he would not let her forget it. 'You will wear what I say you will wear,' he said, nailing her with his gaze. 'Do you understand?'

Her eyes flashed like fire. 'Does it make you feel big and macho and tough to force me to do what you want?' she asked. 'Does it make you feel big and powerful and invincible?'

It made him feel terrible inside, but he wasn't going to tell her that. 'I want our wedding day to be a day to remember,' he said with forced calm. 'I will not have you spoiling it by childish displays of temper or passive aggressive actions that will upset other people who are near and dear to me. You are a mature adult. I expect you to act like one.'

She gave him a livid glare. 'Will that be all, master?' she asked.

He pushed back from the table and tossed his napkin

to one side. 'I'll see you at the chapel on Saturday,' he said. 'I have business to see to until then.'

Her expression lost some of its intractability. 'You mean you're leaving me here…alone?'

'My parents will be here.'

Her throat rose and fell over the tiniest of swallows. 'This is rather sudden, isn't it?' she said. 'You said nothing to me about having to go away on business. I thought you were going to be glued to my side in case I did a last-minute runner.'

Angelo leaned his hands on the table and looked her square in the eyes. 'Don't even think about it, Natalie,' he said through tight lips. 'You put one foot out of place and I'll come down like a ton of bricks on your brother. He will never go to Harvard. He will never go to any university. It will be years before he sees the light of day again. Do I make myself clear?'

She blinked at him, her eyes as wide as big blue saucers. 'Perfectly,' she said in a hollow voice.

He held her pinned there with his gaze for a couple of chugging heartbeats before he straightened and adjusted his tie. 'Try and stay out of trouble,' he said. 'I'll call you later. *Ciao.*'

CHAPTER SIX

THE private chapel at Angelo's grandparents' villa forty-five minutes outside of Rome was full to overflowing when Natalie arrived in the limousine with her father. The last few days had passed in a blur of activity as wedding preparations had been made. She had gone with the flow of things—not wanting to upset Angelo's parents, who had gone out of their way to make her feel welcome.

She had talked to Angelo on the phone each day, but he had seemed distant and uncommunicative and the calls hadn't lasted more than a minute or two at most. There had been no sign of the gentle and caring man she had glimpsed the other night. She wondered if he was having second thoughts about marrying her now he had an inkling of how seriously screwed up she really was.

Her parents had flown over the day before, and her father had immediately stepped into his public role of devoted father. Her mother was her usual decorative self, dressed in diamonds and designer clothes with a hint of brandy on her breath that no amount of mints could disguise.

Her father helped Natalie out of the car outside the chapel. 'You've done well for yourself,' he said. 'I thought you'd end up with some tradesman from the suburbs. Angelo Bellandini is quite a catch. It's a pity he's Italian, but his money more than makes up for that. I didn't know you had it in you to land such a big fish.'

She gave him an embittered look. 'I suppose I really should thank you, shouldn't I? After all, you're the one who reeled him in for me.'

Her father's eyes became cold and hard and his voice lowered to a harsh, dressing-down rasp. 'What else was I to do, you stupid little cow?' he asked. 'Your brother's future depended on getting on the right side of Bellandini. I'm just relieved he wanted to take you on again. Quite frankly, I don't know why he can be bothered. You're not exactly ideal wife material. You've got too much attitude. You've been like that since the day you were born.'

Natalie ground her teeth as she walked to the chapel along a gravelled pathway on her father's arm. She had learned long ago not to answer back. The words would be locked inside her burning throat just like every other word she had suppressed in the past.

They ate at her insides like bitter, poisonous acid.

Angelo blinked when he saw Natalie come into the chapel. His heart did a funny little jump in his chest as he saw her move down the aisle. She was wearing a gorgeous crystal-encrusted ivory wedding gown that skimmed her slim curves. It had a small train that floated behind her, making her appear almost ethereal, and she was wearing a short gossamer veil with a princess tiara that didn't quite disguise the chalk-white paleness of her face. She looked at him as she walked towards him, but he wasn't sure she was actually seeing him. She had a faraway look in her eyes—a haunted look that made him feel guilty for having engineered things the way he had.

He took both of her hands in his as she drew close. They were ice-cold. 'You look beautiful,' he said.

She moved her lips but there was no way he could call it a smile.

'Your mother chose the dress,' she said.

'I like the veil.'

'It keeps the flies off.'

He smiled and gave her hands a little squeeze as the priest moved forward to address the congregation. He felt her fingers tremble against his, and for the briefest moment she clung to him, as if looking for support. But then her fingers became still and lifeless in the cage of his hands.

'Dearly beloved,' the priest began.

'...and now you may kiss the bride.'

Natalie held her breath as Angelo slowly raised her veil. She blinked away an unexpected tear. She had been determined not to be moved by the simple service, but somehow the words had struck a chord deep inside her. The promises had reminded her of all she secretly longed for: lifelong love, being cherished, protected, honoured, worshipped...accepted.

Angelo's mouth came down and gently pressed against hers in a kiss that contained a hint of reverence—or maybe that was just wishful thinking on her part. Halfway through the service she had started wishing it was for real. That he really did love her. That he really did want to spend the rest of his life with her in spite of her 'attitude problem'.

The thought of her father's hateful words made her pull out of the kiss. If Angelo was annoyed at her breaking away he showed no sign of it on his face. He simply looped her arm through his and led her out of the chapel to greet their guests.

The reception was held in the lush, fragrant gardens at his elderly grandparents's spectacular villa, under a beautifully decorated marquee. The champagne flowed and scrumptious food was served, but very little made it past Natalie's lips. She watched as her father charmed everyone with his smooth urbanity. She watched in dread as her mother downed glass after glass of champagne and talked too long and too loudly.

'Your mother looks like she's having a good time,' Angelo remarked as he came back to her side after talking with his grandfather.

Natalie chewed at her lip as she saw her mother doing a tango with one of Angelo's uncles. 'Deep down she's really very shy, but she tries to compensate by drinking,' she said. 'I wish she wouldn't. She doesn't know when to stop.'

He took her by the elbow and led her to a wistaria-covered terrace away from the noise and music of the reception. Bees buzzed in the scented arras above them. 'You look exhausted,' he said. 'Has it all been too much for you?'

'I never thought smiling could be so tiring,' she said with a wry grimace.

'I should imagine it would be when you're not used to doing it.'

She looked away from his all-seeing gaze. He had a way of looking at her that made her feel as if he sensed her deep unhappiness. He'd used to tease her about taking life so seriously. She had tried—she had really tried—to enjoy life, but hardly a day passed without her thinking of all the days her baby brother had missed out on because of her.

'I like your grandparents,' she said, stepping on tip-toe to smell a purple bloom of wistaria. 'They're so devoted to each other even after all this time.'

'Are yours still alive?' he asked. 'You didn't put them on the list so I assumed they'd passed on.'

'They're still alive.'

'Why didn't you invite them?'

'We're not really a close family,' she said, thinking of all the stiff and awkward don't-mention-what-happened-in-Spain visits she had endured over the years.

Everything had changed after Liam had died.

She had lost not just her younger brother but also her entire family. One by one they had pulled back from her. There had been no more seaside holidays with Granny and Grandad. After a couple of years the beautiful handmade birthday presents had stopped, and then a year or two later the birthday cards had gone too.

A small silence passed.

'I'm sorry I couldn't arrange for Lachlan to be here,' he said. 'It's against regulations.'

She looked up at him, shielding her eyes against the bright sun with one of her hands. 'Where is he?'

'He's in a private clinic in Portugal,' he said. 'He'll be there for a month at the minimum.'

Natalie felt a surge of relief so overwhelming it almost took her breath away. She dropped her hand from her eyes and opened and closed her mouth, not able to speak for a full thirty seconds. She had been so terrified he would self-destruct before he got the help he so desperately needed. She had suggested a clinic a couple of times, but he had never listened to her. She had felt so impotent, so helpless watching him destroy his life so recklessly.

'I don't know how to thank you…I've been so terribly worried about him.'

'He has a long way to go,' he said. 'He wants help, but he sabotages it when it's given to him.'

'I know…' she said on a sigh. 'He has issues with self-esteem. Deep down he hates himself. It doesn't matter what he does, or what he achieves, he never feels good enough.'

'For your parents?'

She shifted her gaze. 'For my father, mostly…'

'The father-son relationship can be a tricky one,' he said. 'I had my own issues with my father. That's one of the reasons I came to London.'

Natalie walked with him towards a fountain that was surrounded by sun-warmed cobblestones. She could feel the heat coming up through her thinly soled high-heeled shoes. The fine misty spray of the fountain delicately pricked her face and arms like a refreshing atomiser.

'You've obviously sorted those issues out,' she said. 'Your father adores you, and you clearly adore and respect him.'

'He's a good man,' he said. 'I'm probably more like him that I'm prepared to admit.'

She looked at the water splashing over the marble dolphins in the fountain and wondered what Angelo would think if she told him what *her* father was really like. Would he believe her?

Probably not, she thought with a plummeting of her spirits. Her father had got in first and swung the jury. He had done it all her life—telling everyone how incredibly difficult she was, how headstrong and wilful, how cold and ungrateful. The one time she had dared to tell a family friend about her father's treatment of her it had backfired spectacularly. The knock-on effect on her mother had made Natalie suffer far more than any physical or verbal punishment her father could dish out.

It had silenced her ever since.

'I guess we should get back to the guests,' she said.

'It will soon be time to leave,' he said, and began walking back with her to the marquee. 'I'd like us to get to Sorrento before midnight.'

Natalie's stomach quivered at the thought of spending a few days alone with him at his villa. Would he expect her to sleep with him? How long would she be able to say no? She was aching for him, and had been since she had walked into his office that day. Her body tingled when she was with him. It was tingling now just from walking beside him. Every now and again her bare arm would brush against his jacket sleeve. Even through the barrier of the expensive fabric she could feel the electric energy of his body. It shot sharp arrows of awareness through her skin and straight to her core. She wanted him as she had always wanted him.

Feverishly, wantonly, urgently.

She was the moth and he was the flame that could destroy her, and yet she just couldn't help herself. But giving herself to him physically was one thing. Opening herself to him emotionally was another. If she showed him everything that was stored away inside her what would she do if he then abandoned her?

How would she ever be able to put herself back together again?

Natalie could barely recall the journey to Sorrento in the chauffeur-driven car. She had fallen asleep before they had travelled even a couple of kilometres. She had

woken just after midnight as the car drew to a halt, to
find her head cradled in Angelo's lap, his fingers idly
stroking her hair.

'We're here,' he said.

She sat up and pushed back her loosened hair. 'I
think I dribbled on your trousers,' she said, grimacing
in embarrassment. 'Sorry.'

He gave her a lazy smile. 'No problem,' he said. 'I
enjoyed watching you.'

The villa was perched high on a clifftop, overlooking the ocean. It had spectacular views over the port of
Sorrento and the colourful villages hugging the coast-
line. With terraced gardens and a ground area twice the
size of its neighbours, the villa offered a level of privacy
that was priceless. Lights twinkled from boats on the
wrinkled dark blue blanket of the sea below. The balmy
summer air contained the sweet, sharp scent of lemon
blossom from the surrounding lemon groves, and the
light breeze carried with it the faint clanging sound of
the rigging on a yacht far below.

Angelo left the driver to deal with their luggage as
he led Natalie inside. 'My hotel development is much
larger than this place,' he said. 'I'll take you there tomorrow or the next day.'

Natalie looked around at the vaulted ceilings and the
panoramic arched windows, the antique parquet and
the original terracotta floors. 'This is lovely,' she said.
'Have you had it long?'

'I bought it a couple of years ago,' he said. 'I like the
privacy here. It's about the only place I can lock myself
away from the press.'

'I suppose it's where you bring all your lovers to
seduce them out of the spotlight?' she said before she
could check herself.

He studied her as he pulled free his loosened tie. 'You sound jealous.'

'Why would I be jealous?' she asked. 'I don't have any hold over you. And you don't have any hold over me.'

He picked up her left hand and held it in front of her face. 'Aren't you forgetting something?' he asked. 'We're married now. We have a hold over each other.'

Natalie tried to get out of his grasp but his fingers tightened around hers. 'What possible hold do I have over you?' she asked. 'You forced me to marry you. I didn't have a choice. Five years ago I made the decision to walk out of your life and never see you again. I wanted to be left alone to get on with my life. But no; you had to fix things so I'd be at your mercy and under your control.'

'Stop it, Natalie,' he said. 'You're tired. I'm tired. This is not the time to discuss this.'

She tugged some more until she finally managed to break free. She stood before him, her chest heaving, her heart pounding and her self-control in tatters.

'Don't tell me to stop it!' she said. '*What* hold do I have over you? You hold all the cards. I know what you're up to, Angelo. I know how men like you think. You'll hoodwink me into falling in love with you and then you'll pull the rug from under my feet when I least expect it. But it won't work because I won't do it. I won't fall in love with you. I *won't.*'

He stood looking down at her with implacable calm. 'Do you feel better now you've got all of that off your chest?' he asked.

Goaded beyond all forbearance, she put her chin up and flashed him a challenging glare. 'Why don't you come and collect what you've bought and paid for right here and now?' she said. 'Come on, Angelo. I'm your little puppet now. Why don't you come and pull on my strings?'

A muscle flickered in his jaw as his dark-as-night gaze slowly moved over her body, from her head to her feet and back again. She felt it peel her ivory gown away. She felt it scorch through her bra and knickers. She felt it burn her flesh. She felt it light an inferno between her legs.

But then a mask slipped over his features. 'I'll see you in the morning,' he said. 'I hope you sleep well. *Buonanotte.*' He inclined his head in a brief nod and then turned and left.

Natalie listened to the echo of his footsteps on the terracotta floor fading into the distance until there was nothing left but the sound of her own erratic breathing…

The bedroom she'd chosen to sleep in was on the third floor of the villa. She woke after a fitful sleep to bright morning sunshine streaming in through the arched windows. She peeled back the covers and went and looked out at a view over terraced gardens. There was a sparkling blue swimming pool situated on one of the terraces, surrounded by lush green shrubbery. She could see Angelo's lean, tanned figure carving through the water, lap after lap, deftly turning at each end like an Olympic swimmer.

She moved away from the window before he caught her spying on him and headed to the shower.

When she came downstairs breakfast had been laid out on a wrought-iron table in a sunny courtyard that was draped on three sides in scarlet bougainvillaea. The fragrant smell of freshly brewed coffee lured her to the table, and she poured a cup and took it to the edge of the courtyard to look at the view over the port of Sorrento.

She turned around when she heard the sound of Angelo's tread on the flagstones as he came from inside the villa. He was dressed in taupe chinos and a white casual shirt that was rolled up past his wrists, revealing strong, masculine forearms. His hair was still damp; the grooves of his comb were still visible in the thick dark strands. He looked gorgeously fresh and vitally, potently alive.

'I thought you might've joined me for a swim,' he said.

'I'm not much of a swimmer,' she said, shifting her gaze. 'I prefer dry land sports.'

He pulled out a chair for her at the table. 'Do you want something hot for breakfast?' he asked. 'I can make you an omelette or something.'

Natalie looked at him in surprise. 'Don't you have a twenty-four-hour housekeeper at your beck and call here?'

'I have someone who comes in a couple of times a week,' he said. 'I prefer my time here to be without dozens of people fussing around me.'

'Oh, the trials and tribulations of having millions and squillions of dollars,' she said dryly as she sat down.

He looked at her with a half-smile playing about his mouth. 'You grew up with plenty of wealth yourself,' he said. 'Your father is a very successful investor. He was telling me about some of the ways he's survived the financial crisis. He's a very clever man.'

She reached for a strawberry from the colourful fruit plate on the table. 'He's very good at lots of things,' she said, taking a tiny nibble.

He watched her with those dark, intelligent eyes of his. 'You don't like him very much, do you?' he asked.

'What makes you say that?' she asked, taking another little bite of the strawberry.

'I was watching you at the reception yesterday,' he said. 'You tensed every time he came near you. You never smiled at him. Not even once.'

She gave a shrug and reached for another strawberry, focussing on picking off the stem rather than meeting his gaze. 'We have what you might call a strained relationship,' she said. 'But then he told you how difficult I was when you had that cosy little chat together, didn't he?'

'That really upset you, didn't it?'

'Of course it upset me,' she said, shooting him a hard little glare. 'He's good at swinging the jury. He oozes with charm. No one would ever question his opinion. He's the perfect husband, the perfect father. He doesn't show in public what he's like in private. You don't know him, Angelo. You don't know what he's capable of. He'll smile at your face while he has a knife in your back and you'll never guess it. You don't *know* him.'

The silence that fell made Natalie feel horribly exposed. She couldn't believe that she had said as much as she had said. It was as if a torrent had been let loose. The words had come tumbling out like a flood. A dirty, secret flood that she had kept hidden for as long as she could remember. Her words stained the air. The contamination of the truth even seemed to still the sweet sound of the tweeting birds in the shrubbery nearby.

'Are you frightened of him, *cara*?' Angelo asked with a frown.

'Not any more,' she said, giving her head a little toss

as she reached for a blueberry this time. 'I've taught myself not to let him have that power over me.'

'Has he hurt you in some way in the past?'

'What are you going to do, Angelo?' she asked with a woeful attempt at scorn. 'Punch him on the nose? Rearrange his teeth for him? Give him a black eye?'

His gaze became very dark and very hard. 'If anyone dares to lay so much as a finger on you I will do much more than that,' he said grimly.

A piece of her emotional armour peeled off like the sloughing of skin. It petrified her to think of how easily it had fallen away. Was this his plan of action? To conquer by stealth? To ambush her by making her feel safe and secure?

To protect her?

'You know, for such a modern and sophisticated man, deep down you're amazingly old-fashioned,' she said.

He reached for her hand. 'You have no need to be frightened of anyone any more, *cara*,' he said. 'You're under my protection now, and you will be while you're wearing that ring on your finger.'

Natalie looked at her hand in the shelter of his. The sparkling new wedding band and the exquisite engagement ring bound her to him symbolically, but the real bond she was starting to feel with him was so much deeper and more lasting than that.

And it secretly terrified her.

She pulled her hand out of his and took one of the rolls out of a basket. 'So, what's the plan?' she asked in a light and breezy tone. 'How are we going to spend this non-honeymoon of ours?'

His eyes continued to hold hers in a smouldering tether that made the base of her spine feel hot and tingly. 'How long do you think you'll be able to keep up this ridiculous pretence of not wanting me?' he asked.

She gave a false-sounding little laugh. 'You had your chance last night and you blew it.'

His eyes smouldered some more. 'I was very tempted to call your bluff last night.'

Hot, moist heat swirled between her legs as she thought of how dangerous and reckless her little taunt had actually been. Was that why she had issued it? Did some subconscious part of her want him to take charge and seduce her?

'Why didn't you?' she asked with a little lift of her brow.

'I don't like being manipulated,' he said. 'You wanted me to take the responsibility away from you. You don't like the fact that you still want me. You've taught yourself not to want or need anyone. It bugs the hell out of you that I stir you up the way I do, doesn't it?'

Natalie tried to push her emotions back where they belonged, but it was like trying to refold a map. She pushed back from the table with a screech of the wrought-iron chair-legs against the flagstones. 'I don't have to listen to this,' she said, slamming her napkin on the table.

'That's right,' he said mockingly. 'Run away. That's what you usually do, isn't it? You can't face the truth of what you feel, so you bolt like a scared rabbit.'

She glowered at him in fury, her fists clenched, her spine rigid. 'I am *not* a coward.'

He came to where she was standing, looking down at her with those penetrating eyes of his. She wanted to run, but had to force herself to stand still in order to discredit his summation of her character.

'How long do you think you can keep running?' he

asked. 'Hasn't anyone ever told you that your feelings go with you? You can't leave them behind. They follow you wherever you go.'

'I don't feel anything for you,' she said through barely moving lips.

He gave a deep chuckle of laughter. 'Sure you don't, Tatty.'

She clenched her teeth. 'Stop calling me that.'

'How are you going to stop me?' he asked with a goading smile.

She stepped right up to him and fisted a hand in the front of his shirt. 'Stop it, damn you,' she said, trying to push him backwards. But it was like a moth trying to move a mattress.

His dark gaze mocked her. 'Is that really the best you can do?'

She raised her other hand to slap him, but he caught it mid-air. 'Ah-ah-ah,' he chided. 'That's not allowed. We can play dirty, but not *that* dirty.'

Natalie felt the stirring of his erection against her, and her body responded with a massive tidal wave of lust. The erotic pulse of his blood thundering against her belly unleashed a deranged demon of desire inside her. She lunged at him, pulling his head down by grabbing a handful of his hair so she could smash her mouth against his. He allowed her a few hot seconds before he took charge of the kiss and pushed through her lips with the sexy thrust of his tongue, claiming her interior moistness, mimicking the intimate possession of hard, swollen male inside soft, yielding female.

She tried to take back control but he refused to relinquish it. He commandeered her mouth with masterful expertise, making her whole body sing with delight. One of his hands drove through her hair to angle her head for better access as he deepened the kiss. His other hand found her breast and cupped it roughly, possessively. Her flesh swelled and prickled in need, her nipples becoming hardened points that ached for the hot wet swirl and tug of his tongue. She moved against him, wanting more, wanting it all.

Wanting it *now*.

Her hands dug into his taut buttocks as she pulled him closer. He was monumentally aroused. She felt the rock-hard length of him and ached to feel him moving inside her. Her inner body secretly prepared itself. She felt the dewy moisture gathering between her thighs. She felt the tapping pulse of her blood as her feminine core swelled with longing. She didn't think she had ever wanted him so badly. She was feverish with it.

Her heart raced with excitement as he scooped her up and carried her indoors. But he didn't take her anywhere near a bedroom. He didn't even bother undressing her. He roughly lifted her sundress, bunching it up around her waist, and backed her towards the nearest wall, his mouth still clamped down on hers. He didn't waste time removing her knickers, either. He simply shoved them to one side as he claimed her slick, hot moistness with one of his fingers.

She gasped against his mouth and he made a very male sound at the back of his throat—a primal sound of deep satisfaction that made all the tight ligaments in her spine loosen. He tortured her with his touch. Those clever fingers got to work and had her shaking with need within moments. She clung to him desperately, her fingernails digging into his back and shoulders as he made her shatter into a million pieces. She sagged against him when the first storm was over. She knew there would be more. There always was with Angelo.

He was never satisfied until he had completely undone her physically.

She reached for the zip on his trousers and went in search of him. Her fingers wrapped around his pulsing steely length. He felt hot and hard and heavy with need. She blotted her thumb over the bead of moisture at his tip and a sharp dart of need speared her. He wanted her as badly as she wanted him. Hadn't it always been this way between them? Their coupling had always been a frenzied attack on the senses. Always fireworks and explosions. Always a mind-blowing madness that refused to be tamed.

He pulled her hand away and quickly applied a condom before pressing her back against the wall, thrusting into her so hard and so fast the breath was knocked right out of her. His mouth swallowed her startled gasp as he rocked against her with heart-stopping urgency.

The pressure built and built inside her again. The sensations ricocheted through her like a round of rubber bullets. It had been *so* long! *This* was what she had craved from him. The silky glide of his hard body, those powerful strokes and bold thrusts that made her shiver from head to foot. Her body was so in tune with his. Everything felt so right, so perfect. Her orgasm came speeding towards her, tightening all her sensitive nerve-endings and tugging at her insides, teasing as it lured her towards the edge of oblivion. She cried out as it carried her away on a rollercoaster that dipped and dropped vertiginously.

She was still convulsing when he came. She felt him tense, and then he groaned out loud as he shuddered and quaked with pleasure, his breathing heavy against her neck where he had pressed his face in that last crazy dash to the finish.

It was a moment or two before he stepped away from her. His expression was impossible to read as he did up his zip and tucked his shirt back into his trousers. Natalie felt a pang for the past—for a time when he would smile at her in a smouldering way, his arms holding her in the aftermath as if he never wanted to let her go.

She quickly suppressed that longing, however. She pushed her dress down and her chin up. 'Was that playing dirty enough for you?' she asked.

His dark, unreadable eyes held hers. 'For now.'

She felt a delicious little aftershock of pleasure ripple through her as his gaze went to her mouth. Was he thinking of how she'd used to pleasure him with it? He had done the same to her; so many times she had lost count. There had been few boundaries when it had come to sex. She had learned how to enjoy her body with him, how not to feel ashamed of its needs and urges. He had opened up a wild, sensual world to her that she had not visited since.

She moved away from the wall, wincing slightly as her tender muscles protested.

His expression immediately clouded with concern. 'Did I hurt you?'

'I'm fine.'

He put a hand around her wrist, his fingers overlapping her slender bones, his thumb stroking along the sensitive skin. 'I'm sorry,' he said. 'I shouldn't have taken things so fast. I should've taken my time with you, prepared you more.'

She gave him a nonchalant shrug and pulled out of his hold. 'Save the romantic gestures for someone you didn't have to pay for.'

A hard glitter came into his eyes. 'Is this really how

you want our relationship to run?' he asked. 'As a point-scoring exercise where we do nothing but attack each other?'

'If you're unhappy with how our relationship runs then you have only yourself to blame,' she said. 'You were the one who insisted on marriage. I told you I'm not cut out for it.'

'I wanted to give you the honour of making you my wife,' he said bitterly. 'But clearly you're much more comfortable with the role of a whore.' He took out his wallet and peeled off a handful of notes. Stepping up to her, he stuffed them down the cleavage of her dress. 'That should just about cover it.'

Natalie took the notes out and tore them into pieces, threw them at his feet. 'You'll need far more than *that* to get me to sleep with you again.'

'You're assuming, of course, that I would want to,' he said. And, giving her a scathing look, he turned and left.

CHAPTER SEVEN

NATALIE spent most of the day in her room. She heard Angelo moving about the villa but she refused to interact with him. She was determined to avoid him for as long as she could. Hunger was a minor inconvenience. Her stomach growled as the clock moved around but still she remained resolute.

It was close to eight in the evening when she heard the sound of footsteps outside her door, and then a light tap as Angelo spoke. 'Natalie?'

'Go away.'

'Open the door.'

She tightened her arms across her body, where she was sitting cross-legged on the bed. 'I said go away.'

'If you don't unlock this door I swear to God I'll break it down with my bare hands,' he said in a gritty tone.

Natalie weighed up her options and decided it was better not to call his bluff this time. She got off the bed, padded over to the door, turned the key and opened the door. 'Yes?' she said with a haughty air.

The lines that bracketed his mouth looked deeper and his eyes, though currently glittering with anger, looked tired. 'Can we talk?' he asked.

She stepped away from the door and moved to the

other side of the room, folding her arms across her middle. She didn't trust herself not to touch him. Her body had switched on like a high-wattage lightbulb as soon as he had stepped over the threshold. She could feel the slow burn of her desire for him moving through her. Her insides flickered with the memory of his possession. It was a funny sensation, like suddenly stepping on an uneven surface and feeling that rapid stomach-dropping free fall before restoring balance.

'Are you all right?' he asked.

She sent him a chilly look. 'Fine, thank you.'

He drew in a long breath and then released it. 'What happened this morning…I want to apologise. What I said to you was unforgivable.'

'You're right,' she said, shooting him another deadly glare. 'And, just for the record, I don't forgive you.'

He pushed a hand through his hair. Judging from the disordered state of it, it wasn't the first time that day he had done so. 'I also want to apologise for being so rough with you.' He swallowed tightly and frowned. 'I thought… I don't know what I thought. Maybe I didn't think. I just wanted you.' His eyes darkened as they held hers. 'I have never wanted anyone like I want you.'

Natalie's resolve began to melt with each pulsing second his eyes stayed meshed with hers. She felt the heat of longing pass between them like a secret code. It was there in his dark as night eyes. It was there in the sculptured contours of his mouth. It was there in the tall frame of his body, pulling her like a powerful magnet towards him. She felt the tug of need in her body; she felt it in her breasts, where they twitched and tingled behind her bra. And, God help her, she felt it rattle the steel cage around her heart.

'Apology accepted,' she said.

He came to her and gently cupped her right cheek in his hand, his eyes searching hers. 'Can we start again?' he asked.

She gave a little frown. 'Start from where?'

His mouth curved upwards. 'Hi, my name is Angelo Bellandini and I'm a hotel and property developer. I'm an only child of wealthy Italian parents. I help to run my father's arm of the business while working on my own.'

She gave a resigned sigh. 'Hi, my name is Natalie Armitage and I'm an interior designer, with an expanding sideline in bedlinen and soft furnishings.' She chewed at her lip for a moment and added, 'And I have a fear of flying…'

His thumb stroked her cheek. 'How old were you when you first got scared?'

'I was…seven…'

'What happened?'

She slipped out of his hold and averted her gaze. 'I'd rather not talk about it with a virtual stranger.'

'I'm not a stranger,' he said. 'I'm your husband.'

'Not by my choice,' she muttered.

'Don't do this, Natalie.'

'Don't do what?' she asked, glaring at him. 'Tell it how it is? You blackmailed me back into your life. Now you want me to open up to you as if we're suddenly inseparable soul mates. I'm not good at being open with people. I've never been good at it. I'm private and closed. It must be my Scottish heritage. We're not outwardly passionate like you Italians. You'll just have to accept that's who I am.'

The touch of his hands on her shoulders made every cell of her skin flicker and dance in response.

'You're much more passionate than you give yourself credit for,' he said. 'I've got the scratch marks on my back to prove it.'

Natalie felt that passion stirring within her. His body was calling out to hers in a silent language that was as old as time itself. It spoke to her flesh, making it tauten and tingle all over in anticipation. She wished she had the strength or indeed the willpower to step back from his magnetic heat, but her body was on autopilot. She pressed closer, that delicious ache of need starting deep in her core.

His mouth came down towards hers as hers came up, and they met in an explosion of sensation that made the flesh on her body shudder in delight. He flooded her senses with his taste—mint and male, heat and primal purpose. His tongue darted and dived around hers, subjecting it to a teasing tango that made her spine shiver and shake like a string of bottle caps rattling against each other. Heat pooled between her legs as he moved against her, the thickened length of him exciting her unbearably. She rubbed against him wantonly, desperate for the earth-shattering release that he alone could give her.

He pulled back slightly, his breathing heavy. 'Too fast.'

'Not fast enough,' she said and, pulling his head down, covered his mouth with her greedy one.

His hands worked on her clothes with deliberate attention to detail. She squirmed and writhed as he kissed every spot of flesh as he gradually exposed it. She tugged his shirt out of his trousers and with more haste than precision got him out of the rest of his clothes. She ran her hands over him reverentially. He was so strong and so lean, his muscles tightly corded, his skin satin smooth all but for the sprinkling of masculine hair that went from his chest in an arrow to his swollen groin. She stroked him with her hand, loving the feel of his reaction to her touch. She heard him snatch in a breath, his eyes glittering as she gave him a sultry look from beneath her lashes.

'If you're going to do what I think you're about to do then this show is going to be over before it gets started,' he warned.

She gave him a devil-may-care look and shimmied down in front of him. 'Then I'll just have to wait until the encore, won't I?'

'*Dio mio*,' he groaned in ecstasy as she took him into her mouth.

She used her tongue and the moistness of her saliva to take him to the brink. She would have pushed him over, but he stopped her by placing his hands on either side of her head.

'Enough,' he growled, and hauled her to her feet.

He carried her to the bed, laying her down and covering her, with his weight supported by his arms to avoid crushing her. His mouth took hers in a searing kiss as his hand caressed her breasts and that aching secret dark place between her thighs.

It was her turn to suck in a breath when he moved down her body to stroke her with his lips and tongue. She felt the fizzing of her nerves as he brought her closer and closer. Her release started far away, and then gathered speed and stampeded through her flesh. She lost herself in a whirlpool of sensation that made her feel weightless and boneless.

She opened her eyes to find him looking at her as he stroked a lazy finger down between her breasts. 'Do you want to finish me off with your hand?' he asked.

She gave him a little frown. 'Don't you want to come inside me?'

'I don't want to hurt you,' he said, gently circling one of her nipples. 'You might still be sore.'

She stroked her hand down his lean stubbly jaw. 'I want you inside me,' she said. 'I want *you*.'

His eyes held hers in a sensual lock that made her belly quiver. 'I'll take it easy,' he said. 'Tell me to stop if it hurts.'

'It's not as if I'm a virgin, Angelo,' she said, with a brittle little laugh to cover her unexpected emotional response to his tenderness. 'I can handle everything you dish out.'

His eyes smouldered as they held hers. 'Don't say you weren't warned,' he said, and covered her mouth with his.

Angelo lay on his side and watched Natalie sleep. From time to time he would pick up a silky strand of her hair and twirl it around one of his fingers.

She didn't stir.

Her stubborn refusal to open her heart to him was like a thorn in his flesh. It was as if she would do anything to stop him thinking she cared about him. He thought back to their break-up, to how she had announced without warning that she was leaving. Her bags had been packed when he'd come home from a three-day workshop in Wales. She had told him she had slept with someone she had met at the local pub. He had stood there in dumbstruck silence, wondering if she was joking.

Their relationship had been volatile at times, but he hadn't really thought she was serious about walking out on him. She had threatened to many times, but he had always thought it was just her letting off steam. He had planned to ask her to marry him that very night. He had wanted to wait until he got back from the workshop so she would have had time to think about how much she had missed him. But then she had shown him a photo on her phone, of her with a man, sitting at the bar, smiling over their drinks. The anger he had felt at seeing the evidence of her betrayal had been like a hot red dust storm in front of his eyes. She had stood there, looking at him with a what-are-you-going-to-do-about-it-look and he had snapped.

He wasn't proud of the words he had flailed her with. He was even more ashamed that he'd pushed her up against the wall like a cheap hooker and given her a bruising parting kiss that had left both of them bleeding.

He shuffled through his thoughts as he looked at her lying next to him like a sleeping angel.

She had *wanted* him to believe she had betrayed him. *But why?*

Hadn't he shown her how much he had loved her? He had said it enough times and shown it in a thousand different ways. She had never taken him seriously. Funny that, since she took life so seriously herself. She rarely smiled unless it was a self-effacing one. He couldn't remember ever hearing her laugh other than one of those totally fake cackles that grated on his nerves because he knew them for the tawdry imitation they were.

Why had she been so desperate to get him out of her life?

He was still frowning when she opened her eyes and stretched like a cat. 'What time is it?' she asked.

'You didn't do it, did you?' he asked.

A puzzled flicker passed through her gaze. 'Do what?'

'You didn't sleep with that guy from the bar.'

She made a business of sitting upright and covering herself with a portion of the sheet. 'I went home with him,' she said after a moment.

'But you didn't sleep with him,' he said. 'You wanted me to think you had. You wanted me to believe that because you knew me well enough to know I would never have let you go for anything less.'

A tiny muscle began tapping in her cheek and her eyes took on a defensive sheen. 'I wasn't ready for commitment. You were pressuring me to settle down. I didn't want to lose my freedom. I didn't want to lose my identity and become some nameless rich man's husband just like my mother.'

'You're nothing like your mother, *cara*,' he said. 'You're too strong and feisty for that.'

She got off the bed and wrapped herself in a silky wrap. 'I don't always feel strong,' she said. 'Sometimes I feel...' Her teeth sank into her bottom lip.

'What do you feel?'

She turned to the dressing table and picked up a brush, started pulling it through her hair. 'I feel hungry,' she said. She put the brush down and swung around to face him. 'What does a girl have to do around here to get a meal?'

Angelo knew it wasn't wise to push her. He had to be patient with her. She was feeling vulnerable and had retreated back to her default position. It was her way of protecting herself.

He only wished he had known that five years ago.

Natalie sat across from Angelo in a restaurant in Sorrento an hour later. He had given her the choice of eating in or out and she had chosen to go out. It wasn't that she particularly wanted to mingle with other people; it was more that she wanted to keep her head when around him. She couldn't do that so well when she was alone with him.

The passion they had shared had stirred up old longings that made her feel uneasy. She was fine with having sex with him—more than fine, truth be told. It was just she knew he would want more from her.

He had always wanted more than she was prepared to give.

How long before he would ask her to think about staying with him indefinitely? Then he would start talking about babies.

His mother had already dropped a few broad hints when she had helped her choose her wedding dress. Natalie's stomach knotted at the thought of being responsible for a tiny infant. She could just imagine how her parents would react if she were to tell them she was having a baby. Her mother would reach for the nearest bottle and drain it dry. Her father wouldn't say a word. He would simply raise his eyebrows and a truckload of guilt would land on her like a concrete slab.

Angelo reached across the table and touched her lightly on the back of her hand. 'Hello, over there,' he said with a soft smile.

Natalie gave him a rueful smile in return. 'Sorry… I'm hardly scintillating company, am I?'

'I don't expect you to be the life of the party all the time, *cara*,' he said. 'It's enough that you're here.'

She looked at his fingers entwined with hers. She had missed his touch so much in the years that had passed. She had missed the way his skin felt against hers, the way he felt under the caress of her hands. She had lain awake at night with her body crying out for

his lovemaking. Her body had felt so empty. So lifeless without the sensual energy he shot through it like
an electric charge.

'What are you thinking?' he asked, stroking the un-
derside of her wrist with the broad pad of his thumb.

She met his chocolate-brown gaze and felt her insides flex and contract with lust. 'Do you want dessert?' she asked.

'Depends on what it is,' he said with a sexy glint.

She could barely sit still in her chair for the rocket
blast of longing that swept through her. 'I'm not in the
mood for anything sweet,' she said.

'What *are* you in the mood for?' Still that same sexy
glitter was lighting his eyes from behind.

'Nothing that takes too much time to prepare.'

'I can be a fast order chef when the need arises,' he
said. 'Tell me what you want and I'll deliver it as fast
as humanly possible.'

Natalie shivered as he came behind her to pull out
her chair for her. The fine hairs on the back of her neck
stood up as his warm wine-scented breath coasted past
her ear. She leaned back against him, just for a brief
moment, to see if he was aroused.

He was.

She smiled to herself and walked out of the restaurant with him, her body already quaking in anticipation.

Angelo had barely opened the door of the villa when
she slammed him up against the wall as if she was
about to frisk him.

'Hey, was it something I said?' he asked.

Her dark blue gaze sizzled as it held his. 'You promised me dessert,' she said. 'It's time to serve me.'

The entire length of his backbone shuddered as she

ran her hand over his erection. 'Who's doing the cooking here?' he asked.

She gave him a wicked look and brazenly unzipped him. 'I want an appetiser,' she said.

It was all he could do to stand there upright as she sank to her knees in front of him. He braced himself by standing with his feet slightly apart. When she was in this mood there was no stopping her. He was just happy to be taken along for the ride.

And what a ride it was.

Fireworks went off in his head. He couldn't have held back if he had tried. She ruthlessly teased and caressed him until he was barely able to stand upright. His skin went up in a layer of goosebumps and his heart raced like a fat retiree at a fun run.

She stood up and gave him a wanton smile that had a hint of challenge to it. 'Top that,' she said.

'I can do that,' he said, and swept her up in his arms.

He took her to the master suite. He dropped her in the middle of the mattress and then pulled her by one ankle until she was right between his spread thighs. He leaned over her, breathing in her scent, his mouth coming down to claim her in a sensual feast that had her shuddering in seconds. She bucked and arched and screamed, and even batted at him with her fists, but he wouldn't let her go until he was satisfied that he had drawn every last shuddering gasp out of her.

She lay back and flung a hand over her eyes, her chest rising and falling. 'OK, you win,' she said breathlessly.

'It was pretty damn close,' he said, coming to lie next to her. He trailed a finger down the length of her satin-smooth arm. 'Maybe we should have a re-match some time soon, just to make sure?'

She rolled her head to look at him. 'Give me ten minutes.'

'Five.'

'You're insatiable.'

'Only with you.'

A tiny frown puckered her brow and she turned her head back to look at the ceiling. 'Have there been many?' she asked after a pause.

'Does it matter?'

She gave a careless shrug, but the tight set of her expression contradicted it. 'Not really.'

'I was never in love with anyone, if that's what you're asking.'

'I'm not.'

He sent his fingertip over the silky smooth cup of her shoulder. 'Is it so hard to admit you care for me?' he said.

She shoved his hand away and got off the bed. 'I *knew* you would do this,' she said in agitation.

'What did I do?'

She turned and speared him with her gaze. 'I don't love you,' she said. 'Is there something about those words you don't understand? I don't love you. I *like* you. I like you a lot. You're a nice person. I've never met a more decent person. But I'm not in love with you.'

Frustration made Angelo's voice grate. 'You don't *want* to love anyone, that's why. You do care, Tatty. You care so much it scares the hell out of you.'

She clenched her fists by her sides. 'I can't give you what you want,' she said.

'I want you.'

'You want more,' she said. 'You've said it from the beginning. You want a family. You want children. I can't give you them.'

'Are you infertile?'

She rolled her eyes heavenwards and turned away. 'I knew you wouldn't understand.'

He came over to her and took her by the upper arms. 'Then make me understand,' he said.

She pressed her lips together, as if she was trying to stop an outburst of unchecked speech from escaping.

He gave her arms a gentle squeeze. 'Talk to me, Tatty.'

Her eyes watered and she blinked a couple of times to push the tears back. 'What sort of mother would I be?' she asked.

'You'd be a wonderful mother.'

'I'd be a total nutcase,' she said, pulling away from him. 'I'd probably be one of those helicopter parents everyone talks about. I would never be able to relax. So much can happen to a child. There's so much danger out there: illness, accidents, sick predators on the streets and online. It's all too much to even think about.'

'Most parents manage to bring up their children without anything horrible happening to them,' he said. 'It's easy to look at what's reported in the press and think that the danger is widespread and unavoidable, but you're disregarding all the positive parenting experiences that are out there.'

'I just don't want to go there,' she said. 'You can't make me. No one can make me. You can't force me to get pregnant.'

'I sure hope you're on the pill, then, because I haven't always used protection.'

'Did you do that deliberately?' she asked with a hardened look.

'No, of course not,' he said. 'You were on the pill in

the past…I just assumed… OK, maybe I shouldn't have. I'm clear, if that's what's worrying you.'

'Yes, well, so am I,' she said. 'It's not like I've been out there much just lately.'

'Have you been "out there" at all?'

She tried to look casual about it, but he saw her nibble at the inside of her mouth. 'A couple of times,' she said.

'What happened?'

She gave him a withering look. 'I'm not going to discuss my sex life with you.'

'Did you have sex?'

She looked away. 'It wasn't great sex,' she said. 'More of a token effort, really. I don't even remember the guy's name.'

'What were you trying to prove?'

She looked at him sharply. 'What do you mean by that?'

'I've noticed you have a habit of using sex when you want to avoid intimacy.'

She pulled her chin back in derision. 'That's ridiculous,' she said. 'What sort of pop psychology is that? Isn't sex all about intimacy?'

'Physical, maybe, but not emotional,' he said. 'Emotional intimacy takes it to a whole different level.'

'That's way too deep for me,' she said, with an airy toss of her head. 'I like sex. I like the rush of it. I don't need anything else.'

'You don't want anything else because you're running away from who you really are,' he said.

'I'm sure you're a great big world expert on emotional intimacy,' she said with a scathing curl of her lip. 'You've had five different lovers in the last year.'

'So you *have* been counting.'

She stalked to the other side of the room. 'The Texan heiress was way too young for you,' she said. 'She looked like she was barely out of the schoolroom.'

'I didn't sleep with her.'

She gave a scoffing laugh. 'No, I can imagine you didn't. You would've kept her up way past her bedtime with your silver-tongued charm.'

Angelo ground his teeth in search of patience. 'I'm not going to wait for ever for you, Natalie,' he said. 'I have an empire that needs an heir. I've felt the pressure of that since I was twenty-one years old. If you can't commit to that, then I'll have to find someone else who will.'

She gave him a stony look. 'That's why you forced me into this farce of a marriage, isn't it?' she asked. 'It isn't just about revenge or nostalgic past feelings. It's a convenient way to get what you want. My brother played right into your hands.'

'This has nothing to do with your brother,' he said. 'This is between us. It's always been between us.'

Her slate-blue eyes were hard and cynical. 'Tell me something, Angelo,' she said. 'Would you have done it? Would you really have sent my brother to prison?'

He returned her look with ruthless determination. 'You're still the only person standing between your brother and years behind bars,' he said. 'Don't ever forget that, Natalie. His future is in your hands.'

She put up her chin, her eyes flashing their blue fire of defiance at him. 'I could call your bluff on that.'

He nailed her with his gaze. 'You do that, sweetheart,' he said. 'And see how far it gets you.'

CHAPTER EIGHT

NATALIE walked out in the moonlit gardens when sleep became impossible. She had tossed and fretted for the past couple of hours, but there was no way she could close her eyes without images of the past flickering through her brain like old film footage.

Tomorrow was the anniversary of her baby brother's death.

The hours leading up to it were always mental torture. Was that why she had practically thrown herself at Angelo, in an attempt to block it from her mind? She hadn't seen him since he had stalked out on her after delivering his spine-chilling threat.

She wanted to test him.

She wanted to see if he really was as ruthless as he claimed to be but it was too risky. Lachlan would have to pay the price.

She couldn't do it.

He had a future—the future that had been taken from Liam. Lachlan didn't just have his own life to live; he had that of his baby brother, too. No wonder he was buckling under the pressure. Who could ever live up to such a thing? Lachlan was his own person. He had his own goals and aspirations. But for years he had suppressed them in order to keep their parents happy. He had no interest in the family business. Natalie could see that, but their father could not or would not. Their mother couldn't see further than the label on the next bottle of liquor.

She gave a thorny sigh and turned to look at the shimmering surface of the pool that had appeared as if by magic in front of her. She generally avoided swimming pools.

Too many memories.

Even the smell of chlorine was enough to set the nerves in her stomach into a prickling panic. Before Liam's death she had loved the water. She had spent many a happy hour in the pool at Armitage Manor, practising what she had learned with Granny and Grandad at the beach at Crail. But after Liam had died the pool had been bulldozed and made into a tennis court.

She had never once picked up a tennis racket.

She looked at the moonlit water; a tiny breeze teased the surface. It was like a crinkled bolt of silver silk.

Had she come out here in a subconscious attempt to find some peace at last? Would she ever find peace? Forgiveness? Redemption?

A footfall behind her had her spinning around so quickly she almost fell into the water behind her.

'Couldn't you at least have said something before sneaking up on me like that?' she asked clutching at her thumping chest as Angelo stepped into the circle of light from one of the garden lamps.

'Can't sleep?' he asked.

She rubbed at her arms even though it was still warm. 'It's not all that late,' she said.

'It's three a.m.'

She frowned. 'Is it?'

'I've been watching you for the last hour.'

She narrowed her gaze. 'Don't you mean spying?'

'I was worried about you.'

She raised a brow mockingly. 'What?' she asked. 'You thought I might do something drastic rather than face the prospect of being tied to you for the rest of my life?'

'I was concerned you might go for a swim.'

Her eyebrow arched even higher. 'Do I have to ask your permission?'

'No, of course not,' he said, frowning. 'I was just worried you mightn't realise the danger of swimming alone late at night.'

A hysterical bubble of laughter almost choked her. 'Yeah, right—like I don't already know that,' she said with bitter irony.

His frown gave him a dark and forbidding look. 'You said you weren't a strong swimmer. I thought I should be with you if you fancied a dip to cool off.'

Natalie hid behind the smokescreen of her sarcasm. 'What were you going to do if I got into trouble?' she asked. 'Give me mouth to mouth?'

The atmosphere changed as if someone had flicked a switch.

His eyes smouldered as they tussled with hers. 'What a good idea,' he said, grasping her by the arms and bringing her roughly against him, covering her mouth with his.

His mouth tasted of brandy and hot male frustration. He was angry with her, but she could cope much better with his anger than his tenderness. He disarmed her with his concern and understanding.

She wanted him mad at her.

She wanted him wild with her.

She could handle that. She could pull against his

push. She could survive the onslaught of his sensual touch if she could compartmentalise it as a simple battle of wills, not as a strategic war against her very soul.

His lips ground against hers as his hands gripped her upper arms, his fingers biting into her flesh. She relished the discomfort. She was in the mood for pain. She kissed him back, with her teeth and her tongue taking turns. She felt him flinch as her teeth drew blood, and he punished her by driving his tongue all the harder against hers until she finally submitted.

She let him have his way for a few breathless seconds before she tried a counter-attack. She took his lower lip between her teeth and held on.

He spun her around, so her back was facing the pool, and with no more warning than the sound of his feet moving against the flagstones he tangled his legs with hers so she lost her footing. She opened her mouth on a startled gasp, fell backwards and disappeared under the water, taking him with her.

She came up coughing and spluttering; panic was like a madman inside her chest, fighting its way out any way it could. She felt the sickening hammer blows of her heart. She felt the acrid sting of chlorine in her eyes. She was choking against the water she had swallowed. It burned the back of her throat like acid.

'You...*you bastard*!' she screamed at him like a virago.

He pushed the wet hair out of his eyes and laughed. 'You asked for it.'

She came at him then. Hands in fists and teeth bared, she fell upon him, not caring if she drew blood or worse. She called him every foul name she could think of, the words pouring out of her like a vitriolic flood.

He simply held her aloft, and none of her blows and

kicks came to anything but impotent splashes against and below the water.

Suddenly it was all too much.

The fight went out of her. She felt the dismantling of her spirit like starch being rinsed out of a piece of fabric. She went as limp as a rag doll.

'Do you give up?' he asked, with a victorious glint in his dark eyes.

'I give up…'

His brows moved together and his smile faded. 'What's wrong?' he asked.

'Nothing,' she said tonelessly. 'Can I get out now? I—I'm getting cold.'

'Sure,' he said, releasing her, his gaze watchful.

Natalie waded to the edge of the pool. She didn't bother searching for the steps. She gripped the side and hauled herself out in an ungainly fashion. She stood well back from the side and wrung her hair out like a rope, and pushed it back over her shoulder. It wasn't cold, but she was shivering as if she had been immersed for hours in the Black Sea.

Angelo elevated himself out of the pool with a lot more athletic grace than she had. He came and stood in front of her, his hand capturing her juddering chin so he could hold her gaze. 'You didn't hurt yourself, did you?' he asked.

She flashed him a resentful look. 'It would be your fault if I had.'

'I would never have pushed you in if I didn't think it was safe,' he said. 'The water is deepest this end.'

She wrenched her chin out of his grasp and rubbed at it furiously. 'What if it had been the other end?' she asked. 'I could've been knocked out or even killed.'

'I would never deliberately hurt you, *cara*.'

'Not physically, maybe,' she said, throwing him a speaking glance.

A little smiled pulled up the corners of his mouth. 'So you're feeling a little threatened emotionally?' he asked.

She glowered at him. 'Not at all.'

His smile tilted further. 'It's the sex, *cara*,' he said. 'Did you know that the oxytocin released at orgasm is known as the bonding hormone? It makes people fall in love.'

She gave him a disparaging look. 'If that's true then why haven't you been in love with anyone since we were together? It's not as if you haven't been having loads and loads of sex.'

His eyes held hers in a toe-curling lock. 'Ah, but there is sex and there is *sex*.' His gaze flicked to her mouth, pausing there for a heartbeat before coming back to make love with her eyes.

Natalie felt her hips and spine soften. She felt the stirring of her pulse, the tap-tap-tap of her blood as it coursed through her veins. It sent a primal message to the innermost heart of her femininity, making it contract tightly with need.

'But you're not in love with me,' she said, testing him. 'You just want revenge.'

He stroked a light, teasing fingertip down the length of her bare arm, right to the back of her hand, before he captured her fingers in his and brought her close to his body. She felt the shock of touching him thigh to thigh like a stun gun. It sent a wave of craving through her that almost knocked her off her feet.

'I love what you do to me,' he said. 'I love how you make me feel.'

She could barely think with his erection pressing

so enticingly against her. Her body seeped with need.
She felt the humid dew of it between her thighs. She
looked up in time to see his mouth come down. She
closed her eyes and gave herself up to his devastatingly sensual kiss.

His lips moved with hot urgency against hers,
drawing from her a response that was just as fiery.
Her tongue met his and duelled with it, danced with
it, mated with it. Shivers of reaction washed over her
body. She pressed herself closer, wanting that thrill of
the flesh to block out the pain of the past.

But suddenly he put her from him. 'No,' he said. 'I'm
not falling for that again.'

Natalie looked at him in confusion. 'You don't want
to…?'

He gave her a wry look. 'Of course I want to,' he
said. 'But I'm not going to until you tell me why you
were out here, wandering about like a sleepwalker.'

Her gaze slipped out of the range of his. 'I wasn't
doing any such thing.'

He pushed her chin up with a finger and thumb. 'Yes,
you were,' he said, his gaze determined as it pinned
hers. 'And I want to know why.'

Natalie felt her stomach churning and her shivering
turned to shuddering. 'I told you. I often have trouble
sleeping,' she said.

His eyes continued to delve into hers. 'What plays
on your mind so much that you can't settle?'

She licked her dry lips. 'Nothing.'

His brow lifted sceptically. 'I want the truth, Natalie.
You owe me that, don't you think?'

'I owe you nothing,' she said, with a flash of her
gaze.

His eyes tussled with hers. 'If you won't tell me then

I'll have to find someone who will,' he said. 'And I have a feeling it won't take too much digging.'

Natalie swallowed in panic. If he went looking for answers it might stir up a press fest. She could just imagine the way the papers would run with it. She would have to relive every heartbreaking moment of that fateful trip. Her mother would be devastated to have her terrible loss splashed all over the headlines. Her father had managed to keep things quiet all those years ago, but it would be fair game now, in today's tell-all climate.

And then there was Lachlan to consider.

How would he feel to have the world know he was nothing but a replacement child? That he had only been conceived to fill the shoes of the lost Armitage son and heir?

She ran her tongue over her lips, fighting for time, for strength, for courage. 'I…I made a terrible mistake…a few years back…' She bit down on her lip, not sure if she could go on.

'Tell me about it, Natalie.'

Oh, dear God, *could* she tell him? How could she bear his shock and horror? Those tender looks he had been giving her lately would disappear. How she had missed those looks! He was the only person in the world who looked at her like that.

'Tatty?'

It was the way he said his pet name for her. It was her undoing. How could one simple word dismantle all her defences like a row of dominoes pushed by a fingertip? It was as if he had the key to her heart.

He had always had it.

He hadn't realised it the first time around, but now it was like the childhood game of hot and cold. He was getting warmer and warmer with every moment he spent with her.

Natalie slowly brought her gaze up to look at him head-on. *This is it*, she thought with a sinkhole of despair opening up inside her. *This is the last time you will ever see him look at you like that. Remember it. Treasure it.*

'I killed my brother.'

A confused frown pulled at his forehead. 'Your brother is fine, Natalie. He's safe and sound in rehab.'

'Not that brother,' she said. 'My baby brother, Liam. He drowned while we were holidaying in Spain...he was three years old.'

His frown was so deeply entrenched on his brow it looked as if it would become permanent. 'How could that have been your fault?' he asked.

'I was supposed to be watching him,' she said hollowly. 'My mother had gone inside to lie down. My father was there with us by the pool, but then he said he had to make a really important business call. He was only gone five minutes. I was supposed to be watching Liam. I'd done it before. I was always looking out for him. But that day... I don't know what happened. I think something or other distracted me for a moment. A bird, a flower, a butterfly—I don't know what. When my father came back...' She gave an agonised swallow as the memories came flooding back. 'It was too late...'

'Dear God! Why didn't you tell me this five years ago?' he asked. 'You never mentioned a thing about having lost a brother. Why on earth didn't you say something?'

'It's not something anyone in my family talks about. My father strictly forbade it. He thought it upset my mother too much. It was so long ago even the press have forgotten about it. Lachlan was the replacement child. As soon as he was born every photo, every bit of clothing or any toys that were Liam's were destroyed or given away. It was as if he had never existed.'

Angelo took her by the upper arms, his hold firm— almost painfully so. 'You were not to blame for Liam's death,' he said. 'You were a baby yourself. Your parents were wrong to lay that guilt on you.'

She looked into his dark brown eyes and saw comfort and understanding, not blame and condemnation. It made her eyes water uncontrollably. The tears came up from a well deep inside her. There was nothing she could do to hold them back. They bubbled up and spilled over in a gushing torrent. She hurtled forward into the wall of his chest, sobbing brokenly as his arms came around her and held her close.

'I tried to find him as soon as I noticed he wasn't beside me,' she said. 'It was barely a few seconds before I realised he was gone. I looked and looked around the gardens by the pool, but I didn't see him. He was at the bottom of the pool. I didn't see him. I didn't *see* him…'

'My poor little Tatty,' he soothed against her hair, rocking her gently with the shelter of his frame. 'You were not to blame, *cara*. You were not to blame.'

Natalie cried until she was totally spent. She told him other things as she hiccupped her way through another round of sobs. She told him of how she had seen Liam's tiny coffin being loaded on the plane. How the plane had hit some turbulence and how terrified she had been that his tiny body would be lost for ever. How she had sat in that wretched shuddering seat and wished she had been the one to drown. How her father had not said a word to her the whole way home. How her mother had sat in a blank state, drinking every drink the flight crew handed her.

She didn't know how much time passed before she eased back out of his hold and looked up at him through reddened and sore eyes. 'I must look a frightful mess,' she said.

He looked down at her with one of his warm and tender looks. 'I think you look beautiful.'

She felt a fresh wave of tears spouting like a fountain. 'You see?' she said as she brushed the back of her hand across her eyes. 'This is why I *never* cry. It's too damn hard to stop.'

He brushed the damp hair off her face, his gaze still meltingly soft. 'You can cry all you want or need to, *mia piccola*,' he said. 'There's nothing wrong with showing emotion. It's a safety valve, *si*? It's not good to suppress it for too long.'

She gave him a rueful look. 'You always were far better at letting it all hang out than me,' she said. 'It used to scare me a bit…how incredibly passionate you were.'

He stroked her hair back from her face. 'I seem to remember plenty of passion on your part too,' he said.

'Yes…well, you do seem to bring that out in me,' she said.

His hands slid down to hers, his fingers warm and protective as they wrapped around hers. 'I think it's high time you were tucked up in bed, don't you?'

Natalie shivered as his gaze communicated his desire for her. 'You want to…?'

He scooped her up in his arms. 'I want to,' he said, and carried her indoors.

Angelo lay awake once Natalie had finally dozed off. It had taken a while. In the quiet period after they had made love she had told him how today was the actual anniversary of her baby brother's death. It certainly explained her recent agitation and restlessness. He thought of her horrible nightmare the other night, how she had thrashed and turned and how worried he had been.

It all made sense now.

He still could not fathom why her parents had done such a heartless thing as to blame *her* for the tragic death of their little son. How could they have possibly expected a child of seven to be responsible enough to take care of a small child? It was unthinkably cruel to make her shoulder the blame. Why had they done it? What possible good did they think it would do to burden her with what was essentially their responsibility?

And where had the resort staff been?

Why hadn't Adrian Armitage aimed his guilt-trip on them instead of his little daughter?

His gut churned with the anguish of what she must have faced. Why had she not told him before now? It hurt him to think she had kept that dark secret from him. He had loved her so passionately. He would have given her the world and yet she had not let him into her heart.

Until now.

But she hadn't told him because she had trusted him. He had *forced* it out of her.

He picked up her left hand and rolled the pad of his thumb over the rings he had made her wear.

He had sought revenge, but it wasn't as sweet as he had thought. He hadn't had all the facts on the table. How differently would he have acted if he had known?

His insides clenched with guilt. He had railroaded her into marriage, not stopping to think of the reasons why she had balked at it in the first place. He had not taken the time to understand her, to find the truth about why she was so prickly and defensive. He had not made enough of an effort to get to know her beyond the physical. He had allowed his lust for her to colour everything else.

He had listened to those barefaced lies from her father. Listened and believed them. How could he ever make it up to her? How could he show her there was a way through this if only she trusted and leaned on him?

Or was it already too late to turn things around?

Angelo brought in a tray with coffee and rolls the next morning and set it down beside her. She opened her eyes and sat up, pushing her hair out of her face. 'I don't expect you to wait on me,' she said.

'It's no bother,' he said. 'I was up anyway.'

She took the cup of coffee he had poured for her. 'Thanks,' she said after a little pause.

'You're welcome.'

'I meant about last night,' she said, biting her lip.

Angelo sat on the edge of the bed near her thighs and took one of her hands in his. 'Would you have eventually told me, do you think?'

She lifted one shoulder up and down. 'Maybe—' She twisted her mouth. 'Probably not.'

'I've been thinking about your parents,' he said. 'I'd like to meet with them to talk through this.'

She pulled her hand out of his. 'No.'

'Natalie, this can't go on—'

'No.' Her slate blue eyes collided with his. 'I don't want you to try and fix things. You can't fix this.'

'Look, I understand this is a painful thing for all of you, but it's not fair that you've been carrying this guilt for so long,' he said. 'Your parents need to face up to their part in it.'

She put her coffee cup down with a splash of the liquid over the sides and slid out of the bed. She roughly wrapped herself in a robe and then turned and glared at him. 'If you approach my parents I will *never* forgive you,' she said. 'My mother has enough to deal with. It will destroy her if this is dragged up again. She's barely holding on as it is. And if this gets out in the press it will jeopardise Lachlan's recovery for sure.'

'I'm concerned about you—not your mother or brother,' he said.

'If you're truly concerned about me then you'll do what I ask.'

Angelo frowned. 'Why are you so determined to take the rap for something that was clearly not your fault?'

'It *was* my fault,' she said. 'I was supposed to be watching him.'

'You were a *child*, Natalie,' he said. 'A child of seven should not be left in charge of a toddler—especially around water. How would you have got him out even if you had seen him in time?'

Her features gave a spasm of pain. 'I would have jumped in and helped him.'

'And very likely drowned as well,' he said. 'You were too young to do anything.'

'I could've thrown him something to hold on to until help came,' she said, her eyes glittering with unshed tears.

'*Cara*,' he said, taking a step towards her.

'No,' she said, holding him off with her hands held up like twin stop signs. 'Don't come near me.'

He ignored her and put his hands on her shoulders. She began to push against his chest but somehow as he pulled her closer and she gripped his shirt instead. He brought his head down to hers, taking his time to give her time to escape if she wanted to.

'Don't fight me, *mia piccola*,' he said. 'I'm not your enemy.'

'I'm not fighting you,' she said, her gaze locked on his mouth. 'I'm fighting myself.'

He brushed her mouth with his thumb. 'That's what I thought.'

She gave him a rueful look. 'I can't seem to help myself.'

'You know something?' he said. 'Nor can I.' And then he covered her mouth with his.

CHAPTER NINE

A FEW days later Natalie was wandering around the renovation site of Angelo's hotel development, taking copious notes and snapping photographs as she went along. It was a spectacular development—a wonderful and decadent mix between a boutique hotel and a luxury health spa. Gold and polished marble adorned every surface. Tall arched windows looked out over the sea, or lemon groves and steep hills beyond framed the view. She couldn't believe he was giving her the work. It was a dream job. It would stretch her creatively, but it would springboard her to the heights of interior design.

'Are you nearly done?' Angelo asked as he joined her, after speaking to one of his foremen.

'Are you kidding?' she said. 'I've barely started. This place is amazing. I have so many ideas my head is buzzing.'

He put a gentle hand on the nape of her neck, making an instant shiver course down her spine. 'I don't want you to work too hard,' he said. 'We're supposed to be on honeymoon, remember?'

How could she forget? Her body was still humming with the aftershocks of his passionate possession first thing that morning.

Over the last few days Angelo had been incredibly

tender with her. She was finding it harder and harder
to keep her emotions in check. He was unravelling her
bit by bit, taking down her defences with every kiss and
caress. The same blistering passion was there, but with
it was a new element that took their lovemaking to a
different level—one she had not experienced with him
before. She wasn't ready to admit she loved him. Not
even to herself. She knew she admired and respected
him. She liked being with him and enjoyed being challenged by his quick intellect and razor-sharp wit.

But as for being in love…well, what was the point of
even going there? She could not stay with him for ever.
He had already told her what he wanted. He would not
choose her over his desire for heirs.

'You have a one-track mind, Angelo,' she said in
mock reproach.

He smiled a lazy smile and pressed a kiss to her bare
shoulder. 'Are you going to deny you weren't just thinking about what we got up to this morning?' he asked.

Her belly shifted like a drawer pulled out too quickly
as she thought of how he had made her scream with
pleasure. 'Stop it,' she said in an undertone. 'The work-
men will hear you.'

'So what if they do?' he said, nibbling on her earlobe.
'I am a man in love with his wife. Am I not allowed to
tell the world?'

Natalie stiffened and pulled away. 'I think I'm just
about done here,' she said. 'I can come back another
time.'

'What's wrong?'

'Nothing.'

'You're shutting me out,' he said. 'I can see it in your
face. It's like a drawbridge suddenly comes up.'

'You're imagining it,' she said, closing her notebook with a little snap.

'I won't let you do this, Tatty,' he said. 'I won't let you pull away. That's not how this relationship is going to work.'

She sent him a crystal-hard little glare. 'How *is* this relationship going to work, Angelo?' she asked. 'You want what I can't give you.'

'Only because you're determined to keep on punishing yourself,' he said. 'You want the same things I want. I know you do. Do you think I don't know you by now? I saw the way you looked at that mother and baby when we had coffee in that café yesterday.'

Natalie gave one of her *faux* laughs. 'I was looking at that mother in pity,' she said. 'Did you hear how loudly that brat was crying? It was disturbing everyone.'

'I saw your eyes,' he said. 'I saw the longing.'

She turned and began to stalk away. 'I don't have to listen to this.'

'There we go,' he said, with cutting sarcasm. 'And right on schedule too. Your stock standard phrase makes yet another appearance. I'm sick to death of hearing it.'

She turned back and looked at him. 'Then why don't you send me on my way so you don't have to listen to it any more?' she asked.

His eyes wrestled with hers, dark and glittering with frustration and anger. 'You'd like that, wouldn't you?' he said. 'You'd like to be let off the emotional hook. But I'm not going to do it. You will be with me until the day I say you can finally go.'

'I'm going back to the villa,' she said with a veiled look. 'That is if that's all right with you?'

He sucked in a harsh breath and brushed past her. 'Do what you like,' he said, and left.

* * *

When Natalie came downstairs at the villa a couple of hours later Angelo was on the phone. He signalled for her to wait for him to finish. He was speaking to someone in rapid-fire Italian, his full-bodied accent reminding her all over again of how much she had always loved his voice. It was so rich and deep, so sexy and masculine it made the skin on her arms and legs tingle.

'Sorry about that,' he said, pocketing his phone. 'I have a development in Malaysia that is proving a little troublesome. The staff member I sent over is unable to fix it. I have to go over and sort it out.'

She set her features stubbornly, mentally preparing for another battle of wills. 'I hope you're not expecting me to come with you,' she said. 'I have my own business interests to see to. I can't be on holiday for ever.'

His expression was hard to read. 'I have made arrangements for you to travel back to Edinburgh this evening,' he said. 'I will fly to Kuala Lumpur first thing tomorrow morning.'

The air dropped out of her self-righteous sails. She stood there feeling strangely abandoned, cast adrift and frightened. 'I see…'

'I'll fly to London with you,' he said. 'I'm afraid I haven't got time to do the Edinburgh leg, but one of my staff will go with you instead.'

'I don't need you to hold my hand,' she said with a hoist of her chin.

His dark brown eyes held hers in that knowing way of his. 'You'd better pack your things,' he said. 'We have to leave in an hour.'

The journey to London was surprisingly not as bad as Natalie had been expecting. Her anger at Angelo was enough of a distraction to keep her from dwelling on her fear. He hardly said a word on the flight. Once he had made sure she was comfortable he had buried his head in some paperwork and architectural plans and barely taken a break for coffee or a bite to eat.

Once they landed he introduced her to his staff member, and with a brief kiss to her mouth was gone.

Natalie watched him stride away as if he had just dumped a particularly annoying parcel at the post office and couldn't wait to get on with his day.

'This way, *Signora* Bellandini,' Riccardo said, leading the way to the gate for her flight to Edinburgh.

'It's Ms Armitage,' she insisted.

Riccardo looked puzzled. 'But you are married to *Signor* Bellandini now, *si*?'

'Yes, but that doesn't mean I no longer cease to exist,' she said and, hitching her bag over her shoulder, marched towards the gate.

Natalie was at her studio a couple of days later, leafing through the paper while she had a kick-start coffee before she opened the doors to her clients. Her eyes zeroed in on a photograph in the international gossip section. It was of Angelo, with his hand on the back of a young raven-haired woman as he led her into a plush hotel in Kuala Lumpur. The caption read: *'Honeymoon Over for Italian Tycoon?'*

A dagger of pain plunged through her, leaving her cold and sick and shaking. Nausea bubbled up in her throat—a ghastly tide of bile that refused to go back down. She stumbled to the bathroom at the rear of the office and hunched over the basin, retching until it was all gone. She clung to the basin with white-knuckled hands, clammy sweat breaking over her brow.

'Are you all right?' Linda's concerned voice sounded outside the door.

'I—I'm fine,' Natalie said hoarsely. 'Just a bit of an upset tummy.'

When she came out of the bathroom Linda was holding the newspaper. 'You know the press makes half of this stuff up to sell papers, don't you?' she said, with a worried look that belied her pragmatic claim.

'Of course,' Natalie said, wishing in this case it were true. How stupid had she been to think Angelo was starting to care about her? He had been playing her like a fool from day one. Reeling her in bit by bit, getting her to pour her darkest secrets out to him and then, when she was at her most vulnerable, swooping in and chopping her off at the knees with his cold-hearted perfidy.

Was this how her mother felt every time her father found a new mistress? How did she stand it? The emotional brutality of it was crucifying.

How could Angelo do this to her? Did he want revenge so much? Didn't the last week mean a thing to him? Had it all been nothing but a ruse to get her to let her guard down? How could he be so cold and calculating?

Easily.

He had never forgiven her for walking out on him. Her rejection of him had simmered for five years, burning and roiling deep inside him like lava building and bubbling up in a long-dormant volcano. He had waited patiently until the time was ripe to strike.

It hurt to think how easily she had been duped. How had she allowed him to do that to her? What had happened to her determination to keep her heart untouched?

Her heart felt as if it had been pummelled, bludgeoned. Destroyed.

'Do you know who the woman is?' Linda asked.

'No,' Natalie said tightly. 'And I don't care.'

'Maybe she's his assistant,' Linda offered.

Assisting him with what? Natalie thought as jealousy stung her with its deadly venom. Her mind filled with images of him in that wretched hotel with his beautiful 'assistant'. Their limbs entangled in a big bed, his body splayed over hers, giving the raven-haired beauty the pleasure it had so recently given *her*.

'Are you all right?' Linda asked again.

'Excuse me…' Natalie raced back to the bathroom.

When Natalie got home after work she wasn't feeling much better. Her head was pounding and her stomach felt as if it had been scraped raw with a grater.

She hadn't heard from Angelo—not that she expected him to contact her. No doubt he would be too busy with his gorgeous little dark-haired assistant. Her stomach pitched again and she put a hand on it to settle it, tears suddenly prickling at the backs of her eyes.

Her phone rang from inside her bag and she fished it out. Checking the caller ID, she pressed the answer button. 'How nice of you to call me, my darling husband,' she said with saccharine-sweet politeness. 'Are you sure you've got the time?'

'You saw the picture.'

Her hand tightened around the phone. 'The *whole world* saw the picture,' she said. 'Who is she? Is she your mistress?'

'Don't be ridiculous, Tatty.'

'Don't you *dare* call me that!' she shouted at him. 'You heartless bastard. How could you do this to me?'

'*Cara.*' His voice gentled. 'Calm down and let me explain.'

'Go on, then,' she challenged him. 'I bet you've already thought up a very credible excuse for why you had your hand on that woman's back as you led her into your hotel for a bit of rest and recreation. And I bet there was more recreation than rest.'

'You're jealous.'

'I am *not* jealous,' she said. 'I just don't like being made a fool of publically. You could have at least warned me this was how you were going to play things. I should've known you would have a double standard. One rule for me, a separate one for you. Men like you disgust me.'

'Her name is Paola Galanti and she's a liaison officer with my Malaysian construction team,' he said. 'She is having some difficulty dealing with a very male-dominated work environment.'

'Oh, so big tough Angelo had to come to her rescue?' Natalie put in scathingly. 'Another damsel in distress to rescue and seduce.'

'Will you stop it, for God's sake?' he said. 'Paola is engaged to a friend of mine. I have never been involved with her.'

'Why didn't you tell me your staff member was female when you told me you had to fly over there?' she asked.

'Because her gender has nothing to do with her position on my staff.'

'You still could have told me, rather than let me find out like that in the press,' she said, still bristling with resentment.

'Thus speaks the woman who didn't tell me a thing about her past until I dragged it out of her.'

Natalie flinched at his bitter tone. She bit her lip and

wondered if she was overreacting. Could she trust him? Could she trust anyone?

Could she trust herself?

'Fine,' she said. 'So now we're even.'

She heard him release a heavy sigh. 'Life is not a competition, Natalie.'

'When are you coming back?' she asked, after a tiny tense silence.

'I'm not sure,' he said, sighing again. 'I have a few meetings to get through. There's a hold-up with some materials for the hotel I'm building. It's all turning out to be one big headache.'

She suddenly thought of him all the way over there, in a steamy hot climate, dealing with language barriers and a host of other difficulties on the top of a decent dose of jet lag. How on earth did he do it? He ran not only his own company but a big proportion of his father's as well. So many people to deal with, so many expectations, so much responsibility.

'You sound tired,' she said.

'You sound like a loving wife.'

She stiffened. 'I can assure you I am nothing of the sort.'

'Missing me, *cara*?'

'Hardly.'

'Liar.'

'OK, I miss the sex,' she said, knowing it would needle him. Let him think that was all she cared about.

'I miss it too,' he said, in a low deep tone that sent a rolling firework of sensation down her spine. 'I can't wait to get home to show you how much.'

She felt the clutch of her inner muscles as if they were already twanging in anticipation. She tried to keep her voice steady, but it quavered just a fraction in spite of her efforts. 'I guess I'll have to be patient until then, won't I?'

'I bought you something today,' he said. 'It should arrive tomorrow.'

'You don't have to buy me presents,' she said, thinking of all the gold and diamonds her father had given her mother over the years—presumably to keep his guilt in check. 'I can buy my own jewellery.'

'It's not jewellery,' he said.

'What is it, then?'

'You'll have to wait and see.'

'Flowers? Chocolates?'

'No, not flowers or chocolates,' he said. 'What time will you be at home? I'm not sure the studio is the right place to have it delivered to.'

Natalie felt curiosity building in spite of her determination not to be out-manoeuvred by him. 'I'm working from home all day tomorrow,' she said. 'I have some design work to do on my next collection. I usually do that at home because I get interrupted too much at the studio.'

'Good,' he said. 'I'll make sure it arrives early.'

'Will you at least give me a clue?'

'I have to go,' he said. 'I'll call you tomorrow evening. *Ciao.*'

She didn't even get a chance to reply as he had already ended the call.

The doorbell rang at nine-fifteen. Natalie answered its summons to find a courier standing there, with a small pet carrier in one hand and a clipboard with paperwork in the other.

'Ms Armitage?' he said with a beaming smile. 'I have a special delivery for you. Could you sign here, please?' He handed her the clipboard with a pen on a string attached.

She took the pen and clipboard after a moment's hesitation. She scribbled her signature and then handed it back. 'What is it?' she asked, eyeing the carrier with a combination of delight and dread.

'It's a puppy,' the courier said, handing the carrier over. 'Enjoy.'

Natalie shut the door once he had left. The pet carrier was rocking as the little body inside wriggled and yelped in glee.

'I swear to God I'm going to kill you, Angelo Bellandini,' she said as she put it down on the floor.

She caught sight of a pair of eyes as shiny as dark brown marbles looking at her through the holes in the carrier and her heart instantly melted. Her fingers fumbled over the latch in her haste to get it open.

'Oh, you darling little thing!' she gushed as a furry black ball hurtled towards her, yapping excitedly, its tiny curly tail going nineteen to the dozen. She scooped the puppy up and it immediately went about licking her face with endearing enthusiasm. 'Stop!' she said, giggling as her cheek got a swipe of a raspy tongue. 'Stop, *stop*, you mad little thing. What on earth am I going to do with you?'

The puppy gave a little yap and looked at her quizzically with its head on one side, its button eyes shining with love and adoration.

Natalie felt a rush of nurturing instinct so strong it almost knocked her backwards. She cuddled the little puppy close against her chest and instantly, irrevocably, fell head over heels in love.

* * *

Angelo checked the time difference before he called. He'd had a pig of a day. His meetings hadn't gone the way he would have liked. He was finding it hard to focus on the task at hand. All he could think about was how much he missed Natalie.

Business had never seemed so tedious. He wasn't sure how it had happened, but in the last week or so making money had become secondary to making her happy. He wanted to see her smile. He wanted to hear her laugh. He wanted to see her enjoy life. God knew she hadn't enjoyed it before now. He wanted to change that for her, but she was so damned determined to punish herself. He still hadn't given up on the idea of confronting her parents. How could she ever be truly free from guilt unless they accepted their part in the tragic death of their son?

He pressed her number on his phone, but after a number of rings it went through to voicemail. He frowned as he put the phone down on his desk. Disappointment weighed him down like fatigue from a fever. His whole day had revolved around this moment and now she hadn't picked up.

He was halfway through a mind-numbing report on one of his father's speculative investments when his phone started jumping around his desk. He reached out and picked it up, smiling when he saw it was Natalie calling him back.

'How's the baby?' he asked.

'She peed on the rug in my sitting room,' she said, 'and on the one in my bedroom, and on the absolutely priceless one in the hall. She would've done worse on the one in the study, but I caught her just in time.'

'Oh, dear,' he said. 'I guess she'll get the hang of things eventually.'

'She's chewed a pair of designer shoes and my sunglasses,' she said. 'Oh, and did I mention the holes in the garden? She's been relocating my peonies.'

Angelo leaned back against his leather chair. 'Sounds like you've had a busy day.'

'She's mischievous and disobedient,' she said. 'Right at this very minute she is chewing the cables on my computer. Hey—stop that, Molly. *Bad* girl. Mummy is cross with you. No, don't look at me like that.' Natalie gave a little tinkling bell laugh—a sound he had never heard her make before. 'I *am* cross. I really am.'

He smiled as he heard an answering yap. 'You called her Molly?'

'Yes,' she said wryly. 'Somehow Fido or Rover doesn't quite suit her.'

'But of course,' he said. 'She comes from a pedigree as long as your arm. Both her father and mother were Best in Show.'

There was a little silence.

'Why a puppy?' she asked.

'I'm away a lot,' he said. 'I thought the company would be nice.'

'I have a career,' she said. 'I have a business to run. I haven't got the time to train a puppy. I've never had a dog before. I have no idea what to do. What if something happens to her?'

'Nothing will happen to her, Tatty,' he said. 'Not while you're taking care of her.'

'What about work?' she asked. 'I can't leave her alone all day.'

'So take her with you,' he said. 'It's your studio. You're the boss. You can do what you like.'

Another silence.

'When will you be back?' she asked.

'I'm not sure,' he said. 'Things aren't working out the way I want over here.'

'How is your assistant?'

'Tucked up in bed with her fiancé,' he said. 'I flew him out to be with her.'

'That was thoughtful of you.'

'Practical rather than thoughtful,' he said. 'She was missing him and he was missing her.'

A longer silence this time.

'Angelo?'

'Yes, *cara*?'

'Thank you for not buying me jewellery.'

'You're the only woman I know who would say that,' Angelo said. 'I thought diamonds were supposed to be a girl's best friend?'

'Not this girl.'

'You're going to have to let me buy you some eventually,' he said. 'I don't want people to think I'm too tight to spoil my beautiful wife with lavish gifts.'

'Being generous with money and gifts is not a sign of a happy relationship,' she said. 'My mother is dripping in diamonds and she's absolutely miserable.'

'Why doesn't she leave your father if she's so unhappy?'

'Because he's rich and successful and she can't bear the thought of going back to being a nobody,' she said. 'She's a trophy wife. She's not his soul mate and he isn't hers. By marrying him she gave up her name and her identity. She's an effigy of who she used to be.'

Angelo was starting to see where Natalie's stubborn streak of independence stemmed from. She was terrified of ending up like her mother—bound to a man who had all the power and all the influence. No wonder she had run at the first hint of marriage from him. No wonder she had fought him tooth and nail when he'd blackmailed her back into his life. He had unknowingly sabotaged his own happiness and hers by forcing her to marry him.

'It doesn't have to be that way between us, Tatty,' he said. 'Relationships are not inherited. We create them ourselves.'

'You created this one, not me,' she said. 'I'm just the meat in the sandwich, remember?'

'Even if Lachlan hadn't provided me with the opportunity to get you back in my life I truly believe I would have found some other way,' he said. 'I'd been thinking of it for months.'

'Why?'

'I think you know why.'

There was another little beat of silence.

'I have to go,' she said. 'Molly is running off with a pen. I don't want ink to get on the rug. Bye.'

Angelo put his phone down and let out a long sigh. His relationship with Natalie was a two steps forward three steps back affair that left both of them frustrated. Was it to late to turn things around? What did he have to do to prove to her he wanted this to work?

Would he have to let her go in order to have her return to him on her own terms?

CHAPTER TEN

A COUPLE of days later Natalie heard the deep throaty rumble of a sports car pulling up outside her house. She didn't have to check through the front window to see if it was Angelo. It wasn't the hairs standing up on the back of her neck that proved her instincts true but the little black ball of fluff that was jumping about, yapping in frenzied excitement at the front door.

She couldn't help smiling as she scooped Molly up in her arms and opened the door. 'Yes, I know,' she said. 'It's Daddy.'

Angelo reached for the puppy and was immediately subjected to a hearty welcome. He held the wriggling body aloft. 'I think she just peed on me,' he said, grimacing.

Natalie giggled. 'What do you expect?' she said. 'She's excited to see you.'

His dark eyes glinted as they met hers. 'And what about you, *cara*?' he asked. 'Are you excited to see me too?'

She felt her body tingle as his gaze read every nuance of her expression. She had no hope of hiding her longing from him. She didn't even bother trying. 'Do you want me to lick your face to prove it?' she asked.

'I can think of other places that would suit me much better,' he said.

An earthquake of need rumbled through her lower body. 'What about Molly?' she asked as he moved towards her.

'What *about* Molly?' he said as he released her hair from the knot she had tied on the back of her head.

'Don't you think she's a little young to be watching us…you know…doing it?'

'Good point,' he said, and scooped the puppy up in one hand. 'Where does she sleep?'

She chewed her lip. 'Um…'

He narrowed his eyes in mock reproach. 'You're not serious?'

'What was I supposed to do?' she asked. 'She cried for ages until I took her to bed with me. I felt sorry for her. She was missing her mum.'

He smiled indulgently and flicked her cheek with a gentle finger. 'Softie.'

'I told you I'd be a hopeless mum,' she said. 'I'd end up spoiling the kid rotten.'

'I think you'd make a terrific mother.'

She frowned and took the puppy from him. 'I'll put her in her carrier in the laundry…'

'Tatty?'

She stilled at the door. 'Don't do this, Angelo.'

'You can't keep avoiding the subject,' he said. 'It's an issue that's important to me.'

She turned around and glared at him. 'I know what you're doing,' she said. 'You thought by giving me a puppy to take care of it would magically fix things, didn't you? But I told you before. You can't fix this. You can't fix *me*. You can't fix the past.'

'How long are you going to keep punishing yourself?' he asked.

'I'm not punishing myself,' she said. 'I'm being realistic. I don't think I can handle being a parent. What if I turn out like my father? Having kids changes people. Some people can't handle it. They lose patience. They resent the loss of freedom and take it out on their kids.'

'You're nothing like your father,' he said. 'I find it hard to believe you are even related to him. He's nothing but an arrogant, selfish jerk. He doesn't deserve to have a daughter as beautiful and gentle and loving as you.'

Natalie felt a warm feeling inside her chest like bread dough expanding. She tried to push it down but it kept rising again.

She wanted to believe him.

She wanted it desperately. She wanted a future with him. She wanted to have his baby—more than one baby—*a family.* But the past still haunted her. Would there ever be a time when it wouldn't?

'I need more time...' she said, stroking the puppy's head as she cradled it against her. 'I'm not ready to make a decision like that just yet.'

He put his hands on her shoulders, his dark chocolate eyes meshing with hers. 'We'll talk about it some other time,' he said. 'In the meantime, I think Molly is just about asleep. It would be a shame not to make the most of the opportunity, *si?*'

She trembled with longing as he gently took the puppy from her and led her upstairs into a world of sensuality she was fast becoming addicted to.

How would she ever be able to survive without it?

Natalie was in the garden with Molly the following afternoon when Angelo came out to her.

'Look, Angelo,' she said excitedly. 'Molly has learned to shake hands. Watch. Shake, Molly. See? Isn't she clever?'

'Very.'

She swung her gaze to his but he was frowning. 'What's wrong?' she asked.

He paused for a moment as if searching for the right words. 'Your mother has been taken ill. She's in hospital. Your father just called.'

Natalie felt the hammer blow of her heart against her chest wall. 'Is she all right?'

'She has an acute case of pancreatitis,' he said. 'She's in intensive care.'

'I—I need to go to her.'

'I've already got my private jet on call at the airport,' he said. 'Don't waste time packing. I'll buy what you need when we get there.'

'But what about Molly?' she asked.

'We'll take her with us,' he said. 'I'll have one of my staff take care of her once we get there.'

The intensive care unit was full of desperately ill people, but none of them looked as bad as her mother—or so Natalie thought when she first laid eyes on her, hooked up to machines and wires.

'Oh, Mum,' she said, taking her mother's limp hand in hers. Tears blinded her vision and her chest ached as if someone seriously overweight was sitting on it.

'I've informed Lachlan,' Angelo said at her shoulder. 'I've sent a plane to collect him.'

She pressed her lips to her mother's cold limp hand. 'I'm sorry, Mum,' she said. 'I'm so sorry.'

Adrian Armitage came back in, after taking a call on his mobile out in the corridor. 'And so you should be,' he said with a contemptuous look. 'This is *your* fault. She wouldn't have taken up drinking if it hadn't been for you.'

Angelo stood between Natalie and her father. 'I think you'd better leave,' he said, in a voice that brooked no resistance.

Adrian gave him a disparaging look. 'She's got her claws into you well and good, hasn't she?' he said. 'I warned you about her. She's manipulative and sneaky. You're a damn fool for falling for it.'

'If you don't leave of your own free will then I will *make* you leave,' Angelo said, in the same cool and calm but unmistakably indomitable tone.

'She killed my son,' Adrian said. 'Did she tell you that? She was jealous of him, that's why. She knew I wanted a son more than a daughter. She killed him.'

'Natalie did not kill your son,' Angelo said. 'She was not responsible for Liam's death. She was just a child. She should never have been given the responsibility of watching over him. That was *your* job. I will not have you blame her for your own inadequacies as a parent.'

Natalie watched as her father's face became puce. 'You *dare* to question my ability as a parent?' he roared. 'That girl is a rebel. She's unmanageable. She won't give an inch. She's black to the heart.'

'That girl is *my wife*,' Angelo said with steely emphasis. 'Now, get out of here before I do something you will regret more than I ever will.'

'Mr Armitage?' One of the doctors had appeared. 'I think it's best if you leave. Come this way, please.'

Angelo's concerned gaze came to Natalie's. 'Are you all right, *cara*?' he asked, touching her cheek with a gentle finger.

'I've always known he hated me,' she said on a

ragged sigh. 'It's true what he said…I overheard him blasting my mother about it when I was about five or so. He wanted a son first. That's why I always felt I wasn't good enough. It didn't matter how hard I tried or how well behaved I was or how well I did at school, I could never be the son he wanted. And then when Liam died… well, that was the end of any hope of ever pleasing him.'

'Some people should never be parents,' he said with a furious look. 'I can't believe how pathetic your father is. He's a coward—a bully and a coward. I don't want you to ever be alone with him. Do you understand?'

Natalie felt another piece of her armour fall away. 'I understand.'

His fierce expression relaxed into tenderness as he cupped her cheek. 'I'm sorry I didn't know what your childhood was like, and even more sorry that you didn't feel you could tell me,' he said. 'The clues were all there but I just didn't see them.'

'I once told a family friend about my father's treatment of me,' she said in a quiet voice. 'It got back to my father. My mother…' She swallowed tightly over the memory. 'My mother drank really badly after that.' She looked back at her mother and gave another sigh. 'I don't want to lose her. I know she's not perfect, but I don't want to lose her.'

He put his hand over hers and squeezed it tightly. 'Then I'll move heaven and earth to make sure you don't.'

Natalie looked physically shattered by the time Angelo escorted her out of the hospital. Her mother showed some signs of improvement, but it was still too early to tell if the severe bout of pancreatitis would settle. The

doctors had told them her mother would not live much
longer unless she gave up drinking.

He put his arm around Natalie's waist as he led her
out to the car he had organised. 'Lachlan should be
here in the morning,' he said. 'In the meantime I think
you should try and get as much rest as you can. You
look exhausted.'

'I don't know how to thank you for everything you've
done,' she said. 'You've been…amazing.'

He put an arm around her shoulders and drew her
into his body. 'Isn't it about time someone stood up for
you?' he said.

'Funny that it's you.'

'Why is that?' he asked.

She gave a little shrug. 'I just thought you'd be the
last person to take my side.'

He pressed a kiss to the top of her head. 'Then you
don't know me all that well, do you?'

Angelo took her to his house in Mayfair. It was an
immaculately presented four-storey mansion, with beautiful gardens in front as well as behind. Wealth and
status oozed from every corner of the building, both
inside and out.

Natalie looked around even though she was almost
dead on her feet. 'This is certainly a long way from that
run down flat we shared in Notting Hill,' she said, once
she had inspected every nook and cranny.

'I liked that flat.'

She gave him a wistful smile. 'Yes, I did too.'

'Come here.'

She came and stood in the circle of his arms. 'You'd
better not tell my twenty-one-year old self about this,'
she said. 'She would be furious with me for obeying
your command as if I had no mind of my own.'

He smiled as he gathered her close. 'I won't tell her if you won't.'

She nestled up against him, loving the warmth and comfort and shelter of his body. She felt like a little beat-up dinghy that had finally found safe harbour during a tempestuous storm.

If only she could stay here for ever.

Over the next few days Natalie's mother improved enough to be moved to the private clinic Angelo had organised. Many years of heavy drinking had caused some serious liver damage. It would be a long road to recovery and, while her mother seemed ready to take the first tentative steps, Natalie wasn't keen to put any money on her succeeding. She had seen her mother's attempts to become sober too many times to be confident that this time would be any different.

Lachlan was another story. He seemed determined to get well, and had asked Angelo to send him back to Portugal once he was sure their mother was out of danger. He had started to talk to counsellors about his childhood; about the impossible burden it was to be the replacement child. Natalie could only hope this would be the turning point he needed to get his life back on track.

She hadn't seen her father since Angelo had spoken to him at the hospital. She suspected he was worried about running into Angelo again. It seemed pathetically cowardly to stop visiting his wife just to protect himself, but then, she wouldn't be able to bear to watch him pretending to be a loving, concerned husband when she had personally witnessed all his hateful behaviour over the years that told another story.

On the afternoon when Angelo took Lachlan to the

airport Natalie sat with her mother in the sun room at the clinic. She had brought Molly along, hoping it would lift her mother's spirits, but Isla barely gave the puppy a glance.

'I wonder when your father's coming in?' she asked, checking her watch for the tenth time. 'He hasn't been to see me since I came here.'

Natalie felt frustrated that her mother couldn't or wouldn't see that her father was only concerned about himself. 'Mum, why do you put up with him?' she asked.

'What are you talking about?' Isla said. 'What do you mean?'

'He treats you like rubbish,' Natalie said. 'He's always treated you like rubbish.'

'I know you don't understand, but I'm happy enough with my lot,' her mother said. 'He's a good provider. I don't ever have to worry about working. I have the sort of lifestyle other people only dream of having.'

'Mum, you could divorce him and still be well provided for,' Natalie said. 'You don't have to put up with his bullying.'

'He wasn't always difficult,' Isla said. 'It was better in the early days. It was a dream come true when he asked me to marry him after I found out I was pregnant. We were both so certain you were going to be a boy. I even bought all blue clothes. I was happy to have a daughter, but your father took it very hard. He got better after Liam was born. But then…'

Natalie's eyes watered and her throat went tight. It was always the same. The same wretched anguish, the same crushing guilt. Would there ever be a time when she would be able to move on without it?

'I'm sorry…'

Isla checked her watch again. 'Do you think you could call the nurse for me?' she said. 'I want to go home. I'm sick of being here.'

'Mum, how can you think of leaving?' Natalie asked. 'You're supposed to stay on the program for at least a month.'

Her mother reached past Natalie to press the buzzer for the nurse. 'I belong at home with your father,' she said with an intractable look. 'I don't belong here.'

Angelo pulled up just as Natalie came out of the clinic. She had a deep frown on her forehead and her gait was jerky, as if she was terribly upset and trying her best to hide it. It amazed him how easily he could read her now. It was as if a curtain had come up in his brain. He could sense her mood from the way she carried herself. The very times she needed support she pushed him away. She got all prickly and defensive. He could see her doing it now.

He got out of the car and held open the door for her. 'What's wrong?' he asked, taking the wriggling puppy from her.

'Nothing.'

'Hey,' he said, capturing her chin and making her look at him. 'What's going on?'

Her eyes looked watery, as if she was about to cry. 'I really don't want to talk about it,' she said.

'Tatty, we *have* to talk about things,' he said. 'Especially things that upset us. It's what well-functioning couples do. I don't want any more secrets between us.'

'My mother is going to check herself out,' she said in a defeated tone. 'I can't stop her. I can't fix this. I can't fix her. I can't fix *any* of this.'

He brushed the hair back from her face. 'It's not your mess to fix.'

'I can't believe she thinks more of her position in society than her well-being,' she said. 'She doesn't love my father. She loves what he can give her. How can she live like that?'

'Some people want different things in life,' he said. 'You have to accept that. It doesn't mean you're going to be like that. You have the choice to do things differently.'

She was silent as he helped her in the car. She sat with Molly on her lap, her hands gently stroking her ears, her expression still puckered by a little frown.

'I'm sorry my family's dramas have taken up so much of your time,' she said after a long pause.

'It's not a problem,' Angelo said. 'What about your work? Is there anything I can do to help?'

'No, I've got everything under control,' she said. 'Linda is working on a few things for me. She's really excited about the Sorrento project. I e-mailed her the photos.'

'I know you'll do an amazing job,' he said. 'And my mother is excited about you helping her with the villa at home. It's her birthday next weekend. My father is bringing her to London to go to the theatre. They'd like to have a little celebration with us. You don't have to do anything. I'll get my housekeeper Rosa to prepare everything.'

She gave him a little smile that faded almost as soon as it appeared. 'I'll look forward to it.'

Angelo's parents arrived at his Mayfair house on Friday evening. Natalie had made up a collection of her linens for his mother as a present, but it was Molly that most interested Francesca.

They had barely come through the door when she scooped Molly out of Natalie's arms. 'Come to Nonna,' she said with a beaming smile. 'You will be good training for me, *si*? I can't wait to be a grandmother. I've already bought a new cot for Angelo's old nursery. It will be the first room you can help me redecorate, Natalie. I am so looking forward to it.'

Natalie felt her heart jerk in alarm. She glanced at Angelo, but he was smiling as if nothing was wrong. She felt the walls closing in on her. She felt claustrophobic. Panic rose inside her. She felt it spreading, making her head tight and her stomach churn.

'Got to keep the Bellandini line going,' Sandro said, with a teasing glint in his eye.

'Give us time,' Angelo said with an amused laugh. 'We've barely come off our honeymoon.'

'What if I don't want a baby?' Natalie said.

It was as if she had suddenly announced she had a bomb ticking inside her handbag. Sandro and Francesca stared at her with wide eyes and even wider mouths.

Francesca was the first to speak. 'But surely you can't be serious?'

Natalie tried to ignore Angelo's dark gaze. 'I'm not sure I want children.'

Francesca's face collapsed in dismay. 'But we've longed for grandchildren for years and years,' she said. 'I was only able to have one baby. I would have loved to have four or five. How can you not want to give Angelo a son?'

'Or a daughter,' Sandro said.

Angelo put his arm around Natalie's waist. 'This is a discussion Natalie and I should be having on our own.'

Francesca looked as if she was about to cry. 'You must make her change her mind, Angelo,' she said. 'Tell her how important it is to you. Our line of the family will die out with you. You can't let that happen.'

'Natalie is more important to me than carrying on the family line,' Angelo said. 'If she decides she can't face the prospect of having a child then I will have to accept that.'

Natalie saw the disappointment on his parents' faces. She saw a shadow of it in Angelo's expression too, even though he did his best to conceal it. Never had she felt more wretched about her past.

The evening went ahead as planned, but she felt on the outside the whole time. It was painful to watch Angelo's parents trying to enjoy themselves. They were clearly upset and uncomfortable.

She had spoilt his mother's birthday—just as she had spoilt everything else.

It was late by the time Angelo came up to their room. Natalie suspected he had been having a private discussion about her with his parents. The whole time she had been waiting for him she had worked herself into a state about how the conversation might have gone.

They would have been polite but concerned, wondering if he was serious about throwing his life away on a woman who could not give him what he most wanted.

He would have told them he loved her enough for it not to matter, but they would press him to have a re-think.

He had a responsibility.

It was his duty.

'Where have you been?' she asked, even before he had closed the door.

'I was seeing to some business,' he said, tugging at his tie.

'Did your parents tell you to divorce me?' she asked.

He frowned. 'Why would they do that?'

'Because I'm not going to be the breeding machine they so desperately want.'

'Tatty,' he said on a frustrated sigh, 'I think you need to take a step back from this and see it from my perspective.'

'Oh, I see it from your perspective, all right,' she said, throwing him a hard little glare. 'You think over time you'll eventually grind me down. You're working on me bit by bit. First it was Molly. Who knows what's next? A kitten, perhaps? But what if it doesn't work? What if I still don't want children?'

'What I said downstairs is true,' he said. 'You are far more important to me than adding to the family tree.'

Natalie *wanted* to believe him. She wanted to be confident that in two years, five years, even fifty years he would still be saying the same thing. She knew he loved her. He showed it in so many ways. She *felt* his love in his touch. She saw it in his gaze. She saw it now.

He tossed his tie to one side. 'How about you come over here and I'll show you just how important you are?' he said with a smouldering look.

She walked towards him on legs that trembled as desire rushed through her like a powerful drug. She had barely closed the distance between them when he grabbed her by the upper arms and crushed his mouth to hers. The kiss was hot, wet and urgent—just like the need that instantly flooded her. His tongue moved against hers, calling it into a sexy duel that made her senses shout and sing in rapture.

He kept his mouth clamped on hers as he walked

her backwards to the bed. He laid her down and began to rid himself of his clothes, all the while watching her with that slightly hooded I'm-about-to-make-love-to-you gaze of his.

'Aren't you going to take off your clothes?' he asked.

She gave him a sultry look. 'I don't know,' she said. 'Should I?'

'You'd better, if you still want them to be in one piece.'

A hot tingling sensation erupted between her thighs. 'This dress cost me a lot of money,' she said. 'I happen to love this dress.'

His eyes glittered as he came towards her. 'I love that dress too. But I think you look much better without it.'

Natalie shivered as he spun her around on the bed and released the zip at the back of her dress in one swift movement. Her bra and knickers were next, along with her shoes.

She tried to turn around but he laid a flat hand on her shoulder. 'Stay where you are,' he said.

She felt that delicious shiver again as his erection brushed against her bottom. It felt hard and very determined. She gave a little gasp as he entered her in a slick hard thrust that made every hair on her head tremble at the roots. He set a fast pace but she kept up with him. Each rocking movement of his hips, each stabbing thrust, sent another wave of pleasure through her. All her nerves were jumping in excitement. She felt the pressure building to a crescendo. Even the arches of her feet were tensed in preparation. Her orgasm was fast and furious. It rippled through her, making her shudder in ecstasy. He emptied himself with a powerful surge that sent another wave of pleasure through her.

But he wasn't finished with her yet.

He turned her and came down over her, his weight supported on one hand as he used the other to caress her intimately. She threw back her head and writhed in exquisite pleasure as he brought her to the brink before backing off again.

'Please,' she gasped as he ruthlessly continued the sweet torture.

'What do you want?' he asked.

'I want *you*.'

'How much?'

'Too much,' she gasped again.

'That makes two of us,' he said, and took her to paradise again.

Natalie stood beside Angelo as they farewelled his parents the following morning. Francesca and Santo each hugged her in turn, and on the surface they were as warm as ever, but she could tell they were struggling to accept the possibility that they would never hold a grandchild of their own in their arms.

Angelo took her hand as the driver pulled away from the kerb. 'I know what you're thinking.'

'They hate me.'

'They don't hate you.'

'I would hate me if I was them,' she said, pulling out of his hold and walking back inside.

'Tatty.'

She swung around to look at him once he had closed the front door. 'This is how it's going to be for the next however many years. Do you realise that, Angelo?' she asked. 'They're going to look at me with that crestfallen look, as if I've ruined both their lives.'

'You have not ruined anyone's life,' he said, blowing out a breath. 'They'll get used to it eventually.'

She felt a tight ache in her chest at how much he was giving up for her. She hadn't even told him she loved him. She wanted to, but it as if the words were trapped behind the wall of her guilt. She had bricked those three little words away and now she couldn't find them amongst the rubble of what used to be her heart.

'But will *you* get used to it?' she asked. 'What about in a couple of years? Five or ten? What about when all your friends have got kids? What if you hold someone else's baby in your arms and start to hate me?'

His expression tightened. 'I think we should shelve this topic until some other time.'

'Why is that?' she asked. 'Because I've touched on a nerve? Go on. Admit it. I've got you thinking about how it's going to be, haven't I?'

A muscle flickered at the corner of his mouth. 'You really are spoiling for a fight, aren't you?'

'I'm just trying to make sure you've looked at this from every angle.'

'You're the one who hasn't looked at this properly,' he bit back. 'Even now you're still punishing yourself for your brother's death, when it's obvious it's no one's fault but your parents'. They're totally inadequate, and always have been, and yet you continue to take the blame. You *have* to let it go, Tatty. You can't bring Liam back. You owe it to him to live a full life. I am sure if things were the other way around you would never have expected him to sacrifice his own happiness.'

She chewed at her lip. There was sense in what he was saying. She hadn't really thought about what Liam would have done if things were the other way around.

Angelo took her hand again and brought it up to his chest. 'Think about it, *cara*,' he said gently. 'What would Liam want you to do?'

Natalie thought of a newborn baby just like Isabel's. The sweet smell, the soft downy hair, the perfect little limbs and dimpled hands. She thought of a little baby that looked just like Angelo, with jet-black hair and chocolate-brown eyes. She thought of watching him or her grow up, each and every milestone celebrated with love and happiness. She thought of how the bond of a child would strengthen what Angelo already felt for her. Just having Molly had brought them closer. He was just as devoted to the little puppy as she was...

She suddenly frowned and glanced around her. 'Where's Molly?'

'She was here a minute ago,' Angelo said.

Natalie pushed past him. 'Molly?' She ran through the house, up and down the stairs, calling the puppy's name. There was no sign of her anywhere—just some of her toys: one of Angelo's old trainers and a squeaky plastic bone. She tried not to panic. She did all the self-talk she could think of on the hop.

Puppies were mischievous little things.

Perhaps Molly had found something new to chew and was keeping it to herself in a quiet corner.

Or maybe she was asleep somewhere and hadn't heard her name being called.

Puppies were either fully on or fully off.

Natalie came bolting back down the stairs just as Angelo was coming back through the front door. 'Have you found her?'

'She's not out on the street,' he said. 'I thought she might have slipped out when we were saying goodbye to my parents.'

'I can't find her.'

The words were a horrifying echo from the past. The gender had changed, but they brought up the very same gut wrenching panic. It roiled in her stomach like a butter churn going too fast. She felt her skin break out in a clammy sweat. Her heart hammered inside the scaffold of her ribs.

'I can't find her. I can't find her.'

'She's probably with Rosa in the kitchen,' Angelo said.

'I've already searched the kitchen,' she said. 'Rosa hasn't seen her.'

He reached for her arm to settle her. 'Tatty, for God's sake—stop worrying.'

Natalie wrenched her arm out of reach. Her heart felt as if it was going to burst through the wall of her chest. She could hardly breathe for the rising tide of despair and guilt.

It was her fault.

She couldn't even be trusted with a puppy. How on earth would she ever cope with a little baby?

'Tatty, calm down and—'

'Don't tell me to calm down!' she cried as she rushed out to the garden. Her lungs were almost bursting as she dashed along the flagstones to the lap pool in the garden.

The smell of chlorine sent her back in time.

She wasn't in the middle of London as a twenty-six-year-old. She was seven years old and she was in Spain and her little brother was missing. People were running about and shouting. Her father was shouting the loudest.

'Where is he? You were supposed to be watching him. *Where is he?*'

Her legs felt as if they were going to buckle beneath her. She couldn't speak for the thudding of her heart. Her skin was dripping in sweat. She could feel it tracking a pathway between her shoulderblades.

She ran along the edge of the pool, searching, searching, but there was no sign of a little body. There was nothing but a stray leaf floating on the surface.

She clutched at her head with both hands, trying to quell the sickening pounding of panic that had taken up residence inside. She was going to be sick. She felt the bubble of bile rise in her throat and only strength of will kept it down.

She had to find Liam. She had to find Liam. She had to find Liam.

'I've found her.'

Natalie's hands fell away from her head as Angelo appeared, carrying Molly in his arms. He was smiling as if her world hadn't completely shattered all over again.

'Here she is,' he said, holding her out to her.

She pushed the puppy away. 'No, take her away,' she said. 'I don't want her.'

Angelo frowned. '*Cara*, she's fine. She was in the wine cellar. Rosa must have accidentally locked her in when she put some new bottles down there a few minutes ago.'

Natalie tried to get her breathing back under control but she was still stuck in the past. All she could think of was her brother's limp little body being lifted from the pool. She could still hear the sound of water dripping from his shorts, from the T-shirt with the yellow lion on the front. She could hear it landing on the concrete.

She could still feel the accusing glare of the sun. It seemed to shine down on her like a scorching spotlight.

Your fault. Your fault. Your fault.

'Tatty?'

She looked at Angelo and suddenly it was all too

much. She had to get away. She could *not* do this. She could not be here.

'I have to leave,' she said. 'I can't do this any more.'

'Don't do this to me a second time, Tatty.'

'I have to do it,' she said tears welling in her eyes. 'I don't belong in your life. I can't give you what you want. I just can't.'

'We can work through this,' he said.

'*I* can't work through this!' She shouted the words at him as she teetered on the edge of hysteria. 'I can *never* work through this.'

'Yes, you can,' he said. 'We'll do it together.'

She shook her head at him. 'It's over, Angelo.'

His mouth pulled tight. 'You're running away.'

'I'm not running away,' she said. 'I'm taking control of my life. You forced me to come back to you. I didn't have a choice.'

His jaw locked. 'I can still send Lachlan to jail.'

She looked at him, with the puppy snuggled protectively against his chest. 'You're not going to do that,' she said. 'You were never going to do that. I *know* you, Angelo.'

'If you know me so well then you'll know if you walk out now I will never take you back,' he said through tight lips.

She felt the ache of losing him for ever settle like a weight inside her chest. It pulled on every organ painfully, torturously. 'I'm not coming back,' she said.

'Go, then,' he said, his expression closing like a fist.

It was the hardest thing she had ever done to turn and walk away from him. She put one foot in front of the other and willed herself to walk forward while everything in her protested.

Don't go. He loves you. He loves you no matter what.

This is the only chance you'll have at happiness. How can you walk away from it?

She allowed herself one last look as she walked out through the front door a few minutes later, bag packed, flight to Edinburgh booked. He was standing with Molly, who was struggling to break free from his arms and go to her. He had an unreadable expression on his face, but she could see the hint of moisture in his eyes.

She walked out of the door and closed it with a soft little click that broke her heart.

CHAPTER ELEVEN

'I HEAR Angelo's got a new lady-friend,' Linda said about a month later as she leafed through one of the gossip magazines during lunch.

Natalie felt a dagger of pain stab her, but she affected an uninterested expression as she put her untouched sushi in the little fridge. 'Good for him.'

'She looks pretty young,' Linda said. 'And she kind of looks like you. She looks devoted to the puppy. Here—have a look.'

Natalie pushed the magazine aside. 'I have work to do, and so do you.'

Linda pouted. 'Yeah, well, we'd have a lot more work to do if you hadn't quit on Angelo's Sorrento deal. Why would you let personal stuff get in the way of gazillions of pounds?'

Natalie gritted her teeth. 'I need to move on with my life.'

'Seems to me you can't really do that until you put the past behind you,' Linda said. She waited a beat before adding, 'Lachlan told me.'

Natalie frowned. 'You were speaking to Lachlan?'

'He calls me now and again to see how you're doing,' she said. 'He kind of told me about...everything. You know—about your little brother and all.'

'He had no right to talk to you about me.'

'He's worried about you,' Linda said. 'It sounds like he's got his stuff pretty much sorted. He thinks it's time you put your ghosts to rest, so to speak.'

'I've got my stuff sorted.'

'Yeah, so why are you so miserably unhappy?' Linda asked. 'You mope around with no energy. You don't eat. You look like you don't sleep.'

'I'm fine,' Natalie said, willing herself to believe it.

'Why don't you take a few days off?' Linda suggested. 'I've got things under control here. Kick back and have a think about things.'

'I have nothing to think about.'

Linda lifted one neat eyebrow. 'Are you sure about that?'

Natalie blew out a breath and finally came to a decision. She had been mulling it over for days. It would be Liam's birthday in a couple of days. She could at least put some flowers on his grave while she was there.

'I need to visit my parents,' she said. 'I won't be away long—just a day or two.'

'Take all the time you need,' Linda said, closing the magazine.

Her mother was the only one home when Natalie arrived.

'You could've called to warn me,' Isla said as Natalie entered the sitting room where her mother was holding a gin and tonic.

'I didn't think kids had to warn their parents when they were dropping by for a visit,' Natalie said.

'I hear Angelo's got himself a new lover.' Isla twirled her swizzle stick.

'I don't believe he's got a new lover,' Natalie said. 'He's not like Dad. He wouldn't betray me like that.'

'You left him.'

'I know…'

'Why on earth did you walk out on him?' Isla asked. 'He's as rich as Croesus and as handsome as the devil.'

'I can't give him what he wants,' Natalie said. 'I don't think I can have a child after what happened to Liam.'

There was an awkward little silence.

'It wasn't your fault,' Isla said on a little sigh. 'I've never blamed you—not really. I know it might've looked like it at times, but I was scared of what your father would do if I contradicted him. He can be quite nasty, as you well know. It wasn't your fault that Liam drowned. If anyone was to blame it was your father.'

Natalie stared at her mother. 'Why do you say that?'

'Because I had a headache when we came back from the beach and went inside to lie down,' she said. 'He said he'd watch you and Liam out by the pool.'

Natalie frowned. 'But he asked *me* to watch Liam. I remember him saying it. He said he had to make a really important call.'

Her mother gave her a worldly look. 'Do you really think it was *that* important?' she asked.

Natalie's stomach churned as realisation dawned. 'He was calling *his mistress*?'

Her mother nodded. 'One of the many he had on the side.'

'Why did you put up with it?' Natalie asked, choking back bitter tears. 'Why did you let him do that to you?'

'I told you why,' Isla said. 'I was scared of what he would do. I had nowhere else to go. There was nowhere else I wanted to go.'

'But you could've got help,' Natalie said. 'You

could've found a shelter or something. There are places for women to go when they're scared.'

'I don't expect *you* to understand,' Isla said. 'I know you want more from your life, with your fancy career and all, but I'm happy with my life. I have money and security. I would have lost all of that if I'd turned up to a shelter with a couple of kids in tow.'

Natalie stared at her mother as if she had never seen her before. Could her mother *really* be that shallow? Had she really sold her soul for diamonds?

'You don't even *like* him,' she said. 'How can you bear to live with him if you don't like him, much less love him?'

Isla raised one of her thin brows cynically. 'Are you telling me you're in *love* with your billionaire husband?' she asked. 'Come on, Natalie, what you really love is his money and what he can give you. It's what all women love. You're no different.'

'I love *everything* about Angelo,' Natalie said. 'I love his kindness. I love that he still loves me, even after I ran out on him. I love his smile. I love his eyes. I love his hands. I love every bit of him. I even love his family. They're not shallow and selfish like mine. They watch out for each other and take care of each other. They stay together because they want to be together, not just for the sake of appearances. I love him. Do you hear me? *I love him.*'

'You're a fool, Natalie,' her mother said. 'He'll break your heart. Men like him always do. They reel you in with their charm and then leave you high and dry.'

'I don't care if he breaks my heart,' Natalie said. 'It will be worth it just to have him for as long as he wants me.'

If he takes me back, she thought in anguish. *Did he really mean it when he said he never would?*

'And how long will that be?' Isla asked. 'You're beautiful now, but what about when your looks fade and you put on a few pounds and have a few more wrinkles than you'd like? What then, Natalie? Is he going to love you then?'

There was a sound at the door, and Natalie spun round to see her father saunter in.

'You have a hide to show your face here,' he said. 'Do you know what day it is?'

Natalie drew herself up to her full height. 'I do, actually,' she said. 'And I'm on my way to the cemetery now, to pay my respects to Liam. But when I leave I am *not* going to take the yoke of guilt with me. That's your burden, not mine. Liam would want me to move on with my life. He would have wanted me to be happy.'

'You killed him,' her father spat viciously, bits of spittle forming at the corners of his mouth. '*You* killed him.'

'I did *not* kill him,' Natalie said. 'I was too young to be left in charge of him. That was your duty of care—but you were too busy lining up another secret assignation with one of your mistresses.'

Her father's face reddened. 'Get out!' He thrust a finger towards the door. 'Get out before I throw you out.'

Natalie stared him down, feeling powerful for the first time in her life. 'You haven't got the guts to throw me out,' she said. 'You're a pathetic coward who has spent years hiding his guilt behind his innocent daughter. I'm not carrying it any more. I pity you and Mum. You've wasted your lives. You don't know the meaning of the word love.'

'I do love you, Natalie,' her mother said, sloshing her

drink as Natalie headed out through the door. 'I have always loved you. Even when you were born a girl instead of a boy I loved you.'

Natalie looked at her with a despairing look. 'Then where the hell have you been all my life?' she asked, and turned and left.

Angelo was trying to get Molly to use the garden as her toilet rather than the rug in his study. There had been a significant regression over the last month in the puppy's training. He hardly knew what to do with her. The young woman he had employed to train her had come with great recommendations, but had created a press fest that he would have given anything to avoid.

He could only imagine what Natalie was making of it.

He had got through each day that she had been gone with a wrenching ache in his chest. It was much worse than five years ago. He had thought he had loved her then, but now his love for her surpassed that by miles.

He had thrown himself into work, but he had no enthusiasm for building an empire he couldn't share with her.

He didn't care about the children thing.

He just wanted her.

He had wanted to go to her, to beg her to come back to him, but he knew she could only be his if she was free to make the choice to be with him—not because she had to be, but because she wanted to be.

'Signor Bellandini?' Rosa appeared at the back door. 'You have a visitor.'

He frowned irritably. 'Tell them to go away. I told you I don't want to be disturbed when I'm at home.'

'I think you might like to be disturbed in this case,' Rosa said.

Angelo looked past his housekeeper to see Natalie standing there. He blinked a couple of times, wondering if he was imagining her. But Molly clearly didn't have any doubt. She barrelled towards her with an excited yap, ears flapping, tail wagging frenetically. He watched as Natalie scooped her up and cuddled her against her chest.

'She's missed you,' he said before he could stop himself.

'I've missed her too,' she said, kissing the puppy's head.

'So,' he said. 'What can I do for you? Do you want me to sign the divorce papers? Is that why you're here? You could have sent them with your lawyer. You didn't have to come in person to rub it in.'

She set the puppy down at her feet and met his gaze. 'Did you really mean it when you said you would never take me back?' she asked.

Angelo tried to keep his expression impassive. 'Why do you ask?'

She ran her tongue over her lips and lowered her gaze. 'I was just kind of hoping you only said that to make me think twice about walking away.'

'You didn't walk away,' he said. 'You ran away.'

Her teeth snagged her bottom lip. 'Yes, I know… I'm not going to do that any more.'

Angelo was still not ready to let his guard down. 'Why are you here?'

She lifted her eyes back to his. 'I wanted to say…' She took a little breath and continued, 'I wanted to say I love you. I've wanted to say it for ages but I wasn't sure how. I couldn't seem to find the words. They were inside me, but I had to find a way to get them out.'

He swallowed the lump that had risen in his throat. 'Why now?' he asked. 'Why not a month ago?'

'I've talked to my parents since then,' she said. 'It turns out my father wasn't making an important business call that day. He was calling his mistress.'

Angelo frowned. 'And he let you carry the guilt all this time?'

'And my mother,' she said. 'I'm not sure I can forgive either of them. I'm still working through that.'

'I don't think you should ever see or speak to them again.'

'They're my parents,' she said. 'I have to give them the chance to redeem themselves.'

'I wouldn't be holding my breath,' he said. 'You're likely to get your heart broken.'

She looked up at him with a pained look. 'I know you've got someone else,' she said. 'I've seen the papers. I just wanted to tell you because...because...'

'She's a dog trainer,' Angelo said with a little roll of his eyes. 'And not a particularly good one. I don't think she knows a thing about puppies, to tell you the truth.'

Her eyes started to shine with moisture. 'Dogs are easy,' she said. 'It's kids that are difficult. But I reckon a dog is a great way to ease yourself into it.'

He held out his arms and she stepped into them. He hugged her so tightly he was frightened he was going to snap her ribs. 'We don't have to rush into anything you don't feel ready for,' he said. 'I'm just happy to have you back in my life.'

'I'm so sorry for what I've put you through,' she said. 'I love you so much. I couldn't bear to lose you all over again.'

He looked down at her tenderly. 'This last month has been torture,' he said. 'So many times I wanted to pick up the phone and call you. I even drove halfway to Edinburgh but then turned back. I thought if you came back it would have to be because it was the only place you wanted to be. I felt I had to let you go in order to get you back.'

She smiled up at him. 'This is the only place I want to be. Here with you.'

He stroked her face, loving the way her eyes were shining with happy tears instead of sad ones. 'Do you think it's too early in our marriage to have a second honeymoon?' he asked.

She stepped up on tiptoe and linked her arms around his neck. 'Is the first one over?' she asked with a twinkling look.

He smiled as he scooped her up in his arms. 'It's just getting started,' he said, and carried her indoors.

* * * * *

COMING NEXT MONTH from Harlequin Presents®
AVAILABLE DECEMBER 18, 2012

#3107 A RING TO SECURE HIS HEIR
Lynne Graham

Tycoon Alexius is on a mission to uncover office-cleaner Rosie Gray's secrets, but getting up close and personal has consequences!

#3108 THE RUTHLESS CALEB WILDE
The Wilde Brothers
Sandra Marton

When Caleb Wilde's night of unrivalled passion with Sage Dalton results in an unexpected gift, he stops at nothing to claim it!

#3109 BEHOLDEN TO THE THRONE
Empire of the Sands
Carol Marinelli

Outspoken nanny Amy Bannester may be suitable for Sheikh Emir's bed, but the rules of the crown forbid her to be his bride.

#3110 THE INCORRIGIBLE PLAYBOY
The Legendary Finn Brothers
Emma Darcy

Legendary billionaire Harry Finn is formidable in business and devastating in the bedroom. What he wants, he gets... Top of his list? Secretary Elizabeth Flippence!

#3111 BENEATH THE VEIL OF PARADISE
The Bryants: Powerful & Proud
Kate Hewitt

A passionate affair on a desert island wasn't top of Millie Lang's to-do list; but one look at Chase Bryant has her thinking again!

#3112 AT HIS MAJESTY'S REQUEST
The Call of Duty
Maisey Yates

Will tempting matchmaker Jessica agree to Prince Drakos's request? Share his bed before he takes a *suitable* wife?

COMING NEXT MONTH from Harlequin Presents® EXTRA
AVAILABLE JANUARY 2, 2013

#229 SECRETS OF CASTILLO DEL ARCO
Bound by His Ring
Trish Morey
When Gabriella finds herself in alluring Raoul's gothic *castillo,* she knows the key to her lavish prison lies in succumbing to his touch!

#230 MARRIAGE BEHIND THE FACADE
Bound by His Ring
Lynn Raye Harris
It's not easy to divorce a sheikh! Sydney must spend forty nights in the desert—and Sheikh Malik will make sure it's more than worth it....

#231 KEEPING HER UP ALL NIGHT
Temptation on her Doorstep
Anna Cleary
Ex-ballerina Amber knows exactly where noise polluter Guy can put his guitar! But Guy knows a much more exciting use for her sharp tongue!

#232 THE DEVIL AND THE DEEP
Temptation on her Doorstep
Amy Andrews
Forget Johnny Depp...modern-day pirate Rick is pure physical perfection—and just the thing to cure author Stella's writer's block!

HPECNM1212

REQUEST YOUR FREE BOOKS!

2 FREE NOVELS PLUS
2 FREE GIFTS!

PASSION
GUARANTEED
SEDUCTION

YES! Please send me 2 FREE Harlequin Presents® novels and my 2 FREE gifts (gifts are worth about $10). After receiving them, if I don't wish to receive any more books, I can return the shipping statement marked "cancel." If I don't cancel, I will receive 6 brand-new novels every month and be billed just $4.30 per book in the U.S. or $4.99 per book in Canada. That's a saving of at least 14% off the cover price! It's quite a bargain! Shipping and handling is just 50¢ per book in the U.S. and 75¢ per book in Canada.* I understand that accepting the 2 free books and gifts places me under no obligation to buy anything. I can always return a shipment and cancel at any time. Even if I never buy another book, the two free books and gifts are mine to keep forever.

106/306 HDN FERQ

Name	(PLEASE PRINT)
Address	Apt. #
City	State/Prov.	Zip/Postal Code

Signature (if under 18, a parent or guardian must sign)

Mail to the **Reader Service:**
IN U.S.A.: P.O. Box 1867, Buffalo, NY 14240-1867
IN CANADA: P.O. Box 609, Fort Erie, Ontario L2A 5X3

Not valid for current subscribers to Harlequin Presents books.

**Are you a current subscriber to Harlequin Presents books
and want to receive the larger-print edition?
Call 1-800-873-8635 or visit www.ReaderService.com.**

* Terms and prices subject to change without notice. Prices do not include applicable taxes. Sales tax applicable in N.Y. Canadian residents will be charged applicable taxes. Offer not valid in Quebec. This offer is limited to one order per household. All orders subject to credit approval. Credit or debit balances in a customer's account(s) may be offset by any other outstanding balance owed by or to the customer. Please allow 4 to 6 weeks for delivery. Offer available while quantities last.

Your Privacy—The Reader Service is committed to protecting your privacy. Our Privacy Policy is available online at www.ReaderService.com or upon request from the Reader Service.

We make a portion of our mailing list available to reputable third parties that offer products we believe may interest you. If you prefer that we not exchange your name with third parties, or if you wish to clarify or modify your communication preferences, please visit us at www.ReaderService.com/consumerschoice or write to us at Reader Service Preference Service, P.O. Box 9062, Buffalo, NY 14269. Include your complete name and address.

HPI1B

It all starts with a kiss

THE ONE THAT GOT AWAY

KELLY HUNTER

COMING JAN 22!

Check out the new Harlequin series.
Fun, flirty and sensual romances.